THE MAKING OF TOMMY RAFFERTY

Chad Godfrey

Printed in the United States of America

First Printing: September 2019

ISBN-9781695875982

This book is dedicated to Christina, Charlie, and Grant.
I love you.

From Levon Helm to Jerry Garcia, Mick Jagger to Todd Snider,
Biggie Smalls to Slaine and Madchild, I also thank the sublime music
of giants that we borrow to score our lives.

Roaring dreams take place in a perfectly silent mind.
Now that we know this, throw the raft away.

Chad Godfrey

Leaving Linesy

I t was an unblemished Cape Cod day, dark blue waves crashing into the rocky beach below the Popponesset Inn, where we were gathered outside at tables set with fancy glassware and white linens. Behind my tears, I smiled listening to a bartender eulogize my grandmother Jackie. Not her husband, not my father—a bartender. An interesting choice, probably, to someone who didn't know her, but it made perfect sense to me. That was Jackie. The person next to her was no better and no worse. Bartender, doctor, black, gay, dwarf, straight white dude—didn't matter. If you made her laugh and weren't full of either yourself or shit, you got a fair chance to be in her circle.

Jackie had been a Cape Codder of the old guard, smoking Marlboro Reds all day at the beach with her girlfriends while the husbands golfed or made their way down to the Cape from jobs in Boston. She drank Dewar's on the rocks at lunch. Towards the end, she would sit and smoke cigarettes out her bedroom window in the nursing home in Plymouth, just across the Sagamore Bridge but a world away from the gulls and salt breezes of the Cape. I bought cheap bourbon for her to stash under the mattress of one of those hospital beds that help you sit up to watch television. It was our secret. I couldn't break her out of that place and take her back to the beach, but I could at least give her a taste of what life had once been.

Brian the bartender ended by saying, "Never again will a group of well-dressed seventy-year-old women snap dimes and nickels down the bar at a rude New Yorker lady." We all let out a rueful laugh. Because he was right—the end of Jackie and her friends was also the end of an era in Popponesset. Before the well-heeled "212s" from New York started to arrive in the 90s, Poppy was run by the likes of Jackie Rafferty and large Irish catholic families from Boston. But that was over. Some stuffy old hag from Manhattan would never even ask Brian's name, let alone have him eulogize her.

For a month now after Jackie's service down the Cape, I find myself reading and rereading the birthday card she had given me just before she died. Whenever I read it, my throat tightened up and my breath came short and shallow. But I couldn't stop myself from doing it.

Dear Tommy,

Here's $20 to help with groceries. Happy birthday!

Love always,

Jackie

Twenty-five years old. Twenty dollars to help buy groceries.

In the year leading up to losing Jackie, I had been fired from my job for incompetence, threatened with eviction for consistently inconsistent rent payments, had testicular surgery as a result of a misdiagnosis, saw two planes carrying innocent people crash into two huge buildings, buried a friend who'd had a heart attack for no apparent reason, and gone through the latest in a series of doomed, pointlessly hurtful relationships since Emily left me three years ago. Emily, the one I still loved, the one who hadn't called in almost nine months—a fact that was driving me batshit crazy.

My cup of coffee was the highlight of my morning. My first beer around four in the afternoon was the best part of my day. The dot-com bubble had burst about the same time as those planes crashed in New York, and now I was hung out to dry in an impersonal Monster.com era where just getting into the office of the person who could interview me was a full-time job in itself. I had reached a dead end, rock bottom, the end of my rope—pick your cliché; they all applied.

In addition to making me about as sad as a human can be, reading Jackie's card often brought on something that had become a feature of my life in the last couple of years: anxiety attacks. I felt one coming now, and there wasn't a thing I could do about it. This was what happened when I feel the world's pity and judgment on my shoulders: first, my breathing started to go haywire. Anxiety had a way of doing this, of reaching into my lungs and pulling out any good air I might want to use to live, replacing it with panic and fear.

I stood up from my couch, eyes fixated on Jackie's scratchy, shaky handwriting, and I started to hyperventilate and gag.

I knew by now that it was futile to fight. My best approach was to take it head-on, to get on all fours and ask aloud for its best shot, to call it names and swear on its mother's grave, as if an anxiety attack had a mother. Somehow it made me feel like more of a man to get angry. And every ounce of self-esteem and perceived manhood did, of course, matter at this point.

I pushed the coffee table aside and stared at the wood floor as the very act of breathing began to torment me. Each short breath felt like the last I would draw before my heart imploded and I woke up on a fluffy white cloud pleading my paltry case for admittance to Saint Peter. Time stretched out like taffy, each second an hour, a sequence of gasping respirations where life was totally out of my control. This time, it was roughly ten minutes of hell. In other words, an eternity.

When it was over, though, I realized that was the last time I would read Jackie's birthday card. I knew it was time to finally go to California. I'd been thinking about it and talking about it for a few years, in that idle way people who never actually do anything think and talk about their grand plans. I could not, would not, stumble into the next year of existence the same way I'd stumbled out of the last few years. I had a thousand bucks and one half-baked movie script to my name, and that would have to be enough to get me to Los Angeles.

I studied the bare walls, the bulges and stains in the ceiling, the cobwebs in the dirty windows. The leaky toilet ran louder than ever, and I was surprised I even heard it because it had been humming its annoying tune for so long. I listened for Linesy, my "pet" mouse named after former Boston Bruin Kenny Linesman, but he must have been asleep somewhere in the walls. I got to my feet.

I walked over to the framed picture of Emily and me on the mantel above the broken fireplace and decided I'd put it in the front seat of my truck so it wouldn't get damaged in transit. The picture would carry me over until I got to see her in person, until her love restored order to my life again. I shut the front door behind me and tried my best to subdue another anxiety attack. It was rare I'd have two in the same day, but it was even more rare that I would do anything that involved risk with my life. I'd always listened to Jackie and now her card was telling me that it was time to go.

I headed out for an oil change at Anthony's Garage on L. Street, returned to my apartment, and packed everything I owned into my rusty blue 1987 Nissan Pathfinder. It took less than an hour. I was unemployed and my apartment was month-to-month, so my sudden departure would neither inconvenience nor concern anyone, except maybe Linesy, who, I noted with some chagrin, would likely himself end up evicted by the next tenant.

The roadside signs made it official—and officially nauseating—that I was leaving the Boston city limits. My family would not appreciate, nor remotely understand, this rash departure. I had always been a loyal son, brother, and friend, but if I was ever going to be the kind of man who didn't need twenty bucks from his grandmother to help with groceries, I had to leave. For better or worse, it was time.

I decided not to call home with my plans until I reached New York City. That way, if I punked out in the next few hours I could return to Boston without anybody knowing I had left. No one would ever have to know I didn't have the guts to make a better life for myself. Except for me, of course.

I didn't appreciate at the time that my own judgment was far worse than anyone else's could be. That I didn't appreciate that illustrates, as well as anything else, why I had to leave in the first place.

I made a quick stop for peanut butter crackers at a gas station off the highway before merging back onto Route 90 West, aka the Mass Pike, en route to New York City for my first stop. I screwed past the backside of Fenway Park's Green Monster, threw Bob Marley into the CD player, and began to take some quarter-life crisis inventory.

But I found I didn't want to think about making my current life better. All I really wanted was to be young again, and I began to obsess on the thought of youth. As an adult every day had become like the Monday after Labor Day weekend on Cape Cod, when friends and good times fled out of my reach and an empty sadness overwhelmed me. I wanted so badly to go back to being younger again, maybe even all the way back to being 3 years old or so, when I could run mad on the beach in a shit-filled diaper under my mother's watchful eye. Where on earth had the time gone? I felt cheated that I couldn't forever be chasing my first kiss or believing Dad could actually have a go at Mike Tyson.

Over State Lines

Hustling through Connecticut in the Pathfinder, I turned the radio down and rang Jimmy Garvey, my best friend. I almost hoped he wouldn't answer because I wasn't sure I had the words to explain myself. Then again, if anyone would at least try to understand me, that person was Garvey, so I didn't hang up. He answered and we got right to it. Like always.

"Jimbo, I owe you a goodbye in person, man," I said.

"The phone isn't in person," he said.

I thought a moment. "When you're right, you're right."

"California, eh?" he asked. Like I said, Jimmy was my best friend. He knew without having to be told.

"Gotta do it, Jimbo."

Jimmy became more like family when we were twelve, after cancer nabbed his father, which ultimately drove his mother into an emotionally wrecked state that required an assisted living situation. His grandparents moved from Florida to Massachusetts to take care of him, and the poor bastards had their hands full. Growing up, Jimmy was no stranger to an underage drinking bust or a mad dash through the woods with the cops on his heels. He spent most of his time at my house. But his grandparents stuck with him, and in return he loved them something fierce. They both passed away a few years ago in quick succession and that was it as far as family for Garvey. I was the next closest thing.

"You've done it this time, Raff," Garvey said.

"My parents don't know yet, alright?"

"Alright, kid," he said.

I could envision that devilish grin curling up from Garvey's mouth, revealing a chipped front tooth (pond hockey, Bailey's Irish Creme) he'd been meaning to get fixed for nine years or so.

"Jesus, Garvey," was all I could muster as far as an explanation of what I was doing, and why.

But Garvey didn't need an explanation. "If this is what you want, man, you can do it," he said. "Do your thing, Raff."

Garvey's teenage years were so hard on him that he was just fine with a light paycheck and simple lifestyle. Still, he understood that I had an itch to leave Boston and maybe try "that screenwriting thing," as he called it.

"Jimbo, you're my blood, man—"

"I know, Raff. Call me when you get there, alright?"

And that was it. He hung up, and I was alone again. Not just alone, but lonely. Lonely as shit.

When packing the truck I'd put the Lorazepam in the center console for quick access, knowing damn well I'd need it. Now I reached down and shook two into my palm. I tossed them back dry; I'd taken so many the past year, I didn't even need water anymore to swallow the damn things.

As the road carried me further and further from Boston, I wondered if I could survive somewhere else. What would I do without the *Herald* Sports section, a Dunkies regular, Saturday nights with the crew over at Sullivan's in Charlestown? How could I get by without Natalie Jacobsen's local news updates, fishing for stripers off Dad's boat, and knowing my way around the MBTA trains better than Charlie? Boston was the only city I'd known, and as I lost more and more of my identity over time, I suppose I'd taken to borrowing the city's identity as my own. I rolled down the window in my truck to inhale the crisp October air, but it didn't help. What the fuck was I doing, driving clear across the country, with no money, no prospects, and no idea whether I had what it took to actually succeed at "that screenwriting thing"?

Then the Lorazepam hit my synapses, slowing my breath, calming my brain, and I had a thought: you can't steal second base without first taking a lead off first. Dad had taught me that, way back in little league. He was always most comfortable teaching me lessons—just talking wasn't his strong suit. You have to take your lead, he told me. Measure it out. One long side-step. Two, if you were feeling confident. Time the pitcher to the plate. Keep an eye on his hips; everything from there up would lie about his intentions, whether he was throwing to home or to first, but the hips would always give him away. Stealing second isn't about speed, my father told me, it's about preparation and smarts. But eventually, after all that preparation, all that watching the pitcher and waiting for just the right moment, you had to twist your hips towards second and go for it. If you couldn't get to that moment, you'd find yourself still standing on first when the inning was over.

9

I can still hear those words, in my father's voice, all these years later.

Still, this felt a lot more like trying to steal home. And there's a reason why ballplayers almost never try to do that: it's next to impossible.

Even with the drugs onboard, I was still anxious as hell. Nerves frayed, fearful of the traffic whizzing around me, strung out and scared and ready for a drink. Fortunately, I'd called ahead to my old college friend Craigy Stone, and he agreed to let me crash with him for the night in Manhattan. The first leg of my trek finally ended when I identified the neon sign that marked the bar where I was meeting him.

I pulled into a parking garage near the bar and drove up to the attendant's booth. Inside sat a surly-looking Arab who barely acknowledged my presence. He slid the window open, handed over a ticket, and closed the window again, all without saying a word, or even doing me the courtesy of making eye contact.

I don't know why his brusqueness bothered me so much, but it did. I smoldered as I drove up looking for an empty spot. Who did he think he was, treating me so shabbily in my own country? Where did he get off, acting like he had more right to be here than I did? The place where the towers fell was still being cleared, fires still burning underground, and this guy was acting like I was the one who didn't belong. This went on until well after I'd parked the Pathfinder and made my way back down to the street, went on, in fact, until I hit the front door of the bar where Craigy waited for me.

I knew Craigy would be enjoying his favorite drinks simultaneously, as always – a Bud draft and Jagermeister in a snifter.

There was something so comforting to know how predictable this reunion would be.

"Hey everybody, my boyfriend's back!" Craigy, bottle-tanned and fit, shouted as his eyes caught me entering the bar.

He was as loud as ever. Twenty or so pairs of eyes whipped around to find the 'boyfriend' and in an instant I turned red on pale.

What made being the sudden center of attention worse was the fact that I was the only one in the place without business attire and a clean shave. In the bars I frequented in Boston no one wore a tie, and I fit in just fine; here, everyone wore a tie, making my jeans and flannel about as conspicuous as could be. I smiled and saluted Craigy as I approached him at the bar. I felt everyone's eyes still on me and needed reprieve, in the form of an alcoholic beverage, as soon as possible.

"Late as always," Craigy said as he stood to shake my hand and embrace me in a quick hug.

"Long drive, man," I said with a forced smile that I hoped looked genuine.

We sat down. It felt good to have something solid and stationary beneath me, something that wasn't going eighty miles an hour, something I didn't have to steer.

Craigy never had use for small talk, no need to discuss the obvious, so we were deep into conversation about what the hell I was doing and why halfway through my first beer as we waited for cheeseburgers to come out of the kitchen.

"I don't see any problem here, man," he continued. "You're doing the right thing. Follow your dreams."

"I thought you didn't like Emily," I said.

"She's not your dream. She's your nightmare. I'm talking about the screenwriting thing."

Craigy sniffed his Jagermeister as if something about it might be different than the last ten thousand he had slammed.

"Emily's out there, too. Might as well look her up, you know?"

"She's moved on, Raff," he said.

I let it slide, but knew he was wrong.

Our burgers arrived, and I chomped off a huge bite to buy some time and try to calm myself. My pills were in the Pathfinder. I knew I couldn't take much more introspection or I'd probably choke on my burger, drop to my knees, and start screaming for a paper bag to hyperventilate into.

"Okay, your turn. Let's disassemble your existence," I said.

"Whoa now," Craigy said. "I'm perfectly comfortable with it. Listen, Raff, there isn't a soul under thirty who doesn't battle with their own life. Relationships, job changes, school loans, comparisons to friends already making big money, buying houses and having babies – it's *nuts*. Shit, I bet most'd kill to be in your shoes."

"You're kidding, right?"

Craigy was making well over a hundred thousand dollars a year at Morgan Stanley but he was trying to convince me he'd rather be traveling to California with a thousand dollars to his name?

"No joke at all. How many people you know would be doing what they're doing if they didn't get paid for it?"

"Aside from you?" I offered.

12

"I sell bonds, Raff. C'mon."

Maybe he had a point.

We talked and drank, drank and talked, for the better part of the next eight hours, switching bars occasionally, until we eventually ended up late-night back at Craigy's to crash drunk feet to feet on an L-shaped couch. The next morning I woke to the sounds of Craigy getting ready for work—shower running, coffee maker gurgling. I rolled over and dozed until sometime around 7am.

"You up?" he asked.

"Barely," I said, pulling myself into a sitting position, my back against the headboard.

"Better get yourself together and get on the road," he said. "You've got a long way to go."

It was a reminder I neither wanted nor needed.

"Thanks for letting me crash, Craigy," I said. "And for the talk."

"Good luck, Raff."

He rummaged around a minute longer in the kitchen. Then I heard him wish me the best as he shut the door to his apartment. I swung my feet to the floor, confused and thick-headed. I wanted to sleep another five or six hours, but my hangover made the room unbearably stuffy, and besides, Craigy was right—there were a lot of miles left to cover. I couldn't even swallow I was so dehydrated. All the confidence Craigy had passed on to me the previous night was now gone.

Walking up East 38th to get my car, I noticed about ten trailers lined up along the right side of the street. A herd of young Hispanic girls huddled outside one of the trailers, and I walked over to do a little detective work. Before I had a chance to ask who was inside the trailer, the door opened and out came Jennifer Lopez in a maid's uniform.

The Hispanic girls and I giggled and skipped behind her down 38th until she somehow left us in the dust at the intersection with 6th Avenue. This was clearly not the first time she'd made like Houdini. Impressive, really. Now you see me, now you don't.

After the disappearing act we all stood there for a while, wondering what to do next. One of the girls told me J-Lo was filming a movie called "Maid in Manhattan" with Ralph Fiennes, the guy from "Schindler's List." That explained the wardrobe.

Pulling out of the garage, moments after popping a Lorazepam, I approached the attendant's station where the same guy from the day before sat looking every bit as surly as the first time I'd seen him. Now, though, I noticed he had a lapel pin on his jacket: a miniature American flag with the words, "United We Stand". Neither New York City nor the attendant had done me wrong so I handed him a nice tip and nearly apologized for thinking like a racist jerk when I met him.

Two Months

When Dad wasn't policing the suburbs or smoking cigarettes on his boat, he loved to work a shovel or a rake around our property on a Saturday afternoon. We lived in a cul-de-sac neighborhood with families better off than ours, so Dad felt pressured to outdo them all with perfect landscaping. And he did. It was his way of keeping up, and as an adult it struck me as a little weird, a little out of what I knew to be his character—he never really appeared to care what anyone else thought, or to feel any anxiety about his socioeconomic place in the world. But then again, that's one of the things about growing up—you start to understand, through your own experiences and fuck ups, the basic realities of your parents' lives, even the stuff they don't talk about (at least with you): fears and insecurities, failed aspirations and regret.

Dad was graying now and his forearms no longer resembled the barrels of softball bats, but he was still a force I respected. The world was a simple place to him—or at least, that's what I always believed, based on how he acted. There was an order to things. Right was right and wrong was wrong. He stayed on the right side of that line, slept well at night, and never seemed to question any of the choices he'd made in his life. Except, perhaps, for the choice to have me.

I failed to measure up to Dad's example in pretty much every imaginable way, but the way that bothered me the most was my inability to replicate his self-assurance. I felt like a complete embarrassment, to be the son of a stable, respected man while relying on sedatives to keep myself from flipping the fuck out. This was a guy who was so at ease he could reliably fall asleep within two minutes of sitting down in his recliner, while I spent my nights staring at the ceiling, doubting everything I'd ever done, pining away for a girl who'd forgotten me, trying not to let my breathing get out of control.

Dad met Mom through a mutual friend on the Cape when she was there on college break. Eight years later Mom was twenty-seven, the wife of an eager, bullheaded city cop and the mother of two wild towheads. They'd started out in a meager apartment in Quincy about ten miles as the crow flies from the apartment I had just abandoned in Boston. This was before my sister and I came to be. Stacy and I, these aforementioned wild towheads, were both surprises, but Mom was nice enough to make us feel welcome nonetheless.

Mom's personal life vanished with the birth of her children, but she never seemed to need a break or show regret, and she never has. And in that way, she's just like my father: she doesn't have any problem sleeping, either. Like most women raised around Cape Cod in the 60s, my mom loved the Kennedy model of family life, with Jackie O as her Platonic ideal. Husband and children first. Proud wife always second. And she never swayed from it.

When I'd had my first horrific anxiety attack, it was Mom who brought me back to earth over the phone. When I told her I wanted to be a screenwriter, she bought me a book about screenwriting by William Goldman called *Which Lie Did I Tell?*. When Emily left me in a puddle of myself, it was Mom who explained the vagaries of love to me and nearly salvaged my crushed heart. Mom wasn't what you'd call book smart but she had an inborn wisdom about life that I clearly hadn't inherited. I feared her judgment, not because it was harsh, but because it was always right.

Heading out of New York on the Jersey Turnpike, I finally got up the nerve to call home. By this point the Lorazepam had my hangover nicely under control. If I didn't have access to these pills when I was hungover, I went bananas. Hangovers exposed the raw, frightened young man I truly was, making me vulnerable and uncomfortable with anything and everything.

After four infinitely long rings, my mother picked up the phone. I'd been hoping Dad or, even better, the answering machine would pick up. Both would pass the news of her insensitive child onto her clearer and softer than I could.

"Hello?" she said.

"Hey, Mom, it's me," I said, trying to sound upbeat.

"Hi, hun," she said, an odd hesitation in her voice, like she sensed somehow that this wasn't me just checking in.

I rolled down the window to provide a little wind interference, allowing me to slow down the conversation.

"Mom, I'm in New York. New Jersey, actually. I'm on my way out West."

"Thomas, Jesus, Mary and Saint Joseph, are you OK?" she said. "Are you depressed? Should I come get you?"

"No, I'm fine. I'm going to California to see Emily and try writing. Remember how good you thought I could be at that kind of thing?"

"In Boston. Who leaves their mother and father without a good-bye? You should be ashamed."

Good going, Tommy.

"I got shame covered, Ma," I said.

My mother sighed and, to my surprise and dismay, that was the end of our conversation. I wanted to explain myself.

I heard a thunk as she dropped the phone on the table, felt my heart sink as I pictured her walking away without a word. Then, after a moment, I heard a rustle as my father took the phone in one big hand.

"Tommy, what have you done? I swear on Jackie's grave if—"

"Dad, look-

"Remember what I told you after you ran across Fenway in your skivvies?"

"I'm driving to California to get Emily."

I couldn't tell Dad I was leaving for writing. That was hardly a career in the mind of The Chief. Of course, he was no more inclined to view chasing a girl as a good reason to upend my life and, worse, upset my mother.

"For Christ's sake, Tommy," he said, "Why not see if she'll drive three thousand miles for you?"

I'd miscalculated; apparently Emily ranked just below writing on the list of all-time stupid ventures to Dad. I heard him take a deep breath and tell my mother to grab herself a glass of water in the kitchen.

"Tommy, you there?" he asked.

"Yeah, I'm here. But my phone is running low on battery."

"I expect you back here soon. In one piece."

"Sure, Dad," I promised, "Can you just try to make this easier for Mom? She won't hear it from me."

"I'm not the guy to ask for any favors, Tommy. You made your choice, you deal with the fallout. That's how life works." He took a breath. "Call your mother every day. Here she is," he said, and passed the phone back to Mom without hearing me tell him that I loved him. As usual.

"Tommy?" Mom said.

"Yeah, Ma. Look, my phone's dying."

"How much money do you have?" she asked in a whisper, surely trying to keep any talk of financial assistance out of my father's earshot.

"A thousand dollars."

"A *thousand*? That won't get you to California and back, will it?" she gasped. "And what will you do for money when you get there?"

"I dunno. I'm not planning to be back anytime soon, Ma. I'm really doing this. I need to do this."

"I have your bank number still. I get paid next week."

"You don't have to do that."

"I'm your mother, Tommy," she said, as if I needed reminding. "You have to have money. What did you tell your father?"

"Emily."

"Are you trying to kill him, Tommy?"

"You remember what he said when I told him I wanted to be a writer after I graduated?"

"Yeah, 'write' me a check for college, but Tommy-

"Well, there you go then," I said, as if I had clarified the entire mess I was in.

"Take two months, Tommy. You're twenty-five, honey."

"I'll try."

"Get this out of your system. Two months, and then I have to tell your father it's not just a silly charade and the you-know-what hits the fan."

This was not a threat, merely a statement of fact. My father's meager patience for shenanigans were used up. It wasn't going to take much, at this point, for him to write me off completely. And I knew it.

"Thanks for the money, Mom."

"I love you, sweetheart. Drive safe."

I hung up the phone before I started crying, which would make her start crying, which would make my father even more upset than he already was.

I hated on myself the entire way to Cleveland, my next stop. For eight hours, I battled tractor trailers on a two-lane road and tried to convince myself that Craigy's assessment of the move was true and accurate. Everyone wanted to do what I was doing, he'd said. But if that were the case, then why did it upset my parents so much, and moreover, why did it feel so lousy? So stupid, so dangerous, so completely doomed to fail?

Falling in love with Emily was next-level shit. I was eighteen, a freshman in college. It wasn't instantaneous, but when it did finally take Cupid didn't shoot an arrow; he snuck up from behind and clocked me in the back of the head with a 2x4.

At first it wasn't love. It was convenience. It was a girl who did my laundry while I was at baseball practice. It was a girl who looked the other way when she found that bra that didn't belong to her in my laundry basket. Cupid wouldn't give up on me, though, and neither would Emily—at least, not until much later. After a year of dicking around, taking advantage, and taking her for granted, one Saturday morning I rolled over in bed to find Emily lying awake next to me, her blue eyes watching with calm assurance, and it hit me in that moment that she was absolutely perfect. I didn't know where it came from and I didn't know what it meant, but I hadn't been able to imagine a life without her since.

I pulled into Cleveland exhausted and in a sour mood. I was staying with a near-stranger, a guy named Steve Morehead who was a friend of a college friend, and I needed to do my best to not let on how miserable I was.

I knew nothing about Steve, other than that he lived in Lakewood, a modest suburb of Cleveland with a large young graduate population, and that he worked in life insurance sales. I had no problem finding his place, which was fortunate, because I was too tired to read a roadmap in my lap much longer.

"C'mon in," Steve mumbled at the entrance to his house. "I gotta shower up, I'll be ready in ten."

Odd introduction, I thought.

"Ready for what?" I asked.

"Two for one night," he said.

Steve had a plan. I could tell discussion of alternate plans, such as sleep, was not going to happen.

Steve turned away and headed for the showers, leaving me in the doorway with zero instruction on where to put my bags or which bedroom or couch I should claim. I found it odd we didn't shake hands or state our names, instead going straight into plans for discount drinks. I plopped my overnight bag on the couch in the living room kitty-corner to the front door and gave myself the nickel tour.

Everything about Steve's living room decoration was pure macho emptiness. A big dumb Ohio State Buckeyes football banner covered the wall behind the biggest television I had ever seen. Another wall showcased Steve's personal shrine of athletic accomplishments – an all-state football plaque, high school wrestling photos, lacrosse newspaper clippings from his glory days, and so on. The adjacent bookcase, stretching from the ground to the 8-foot ceiling, stored an impressive collection of literature detailing various wars, American politics, and a mess of biographies and life manuals written by athletes, coaches, and historical figures.

I took a seat on the couch and flipped through a recent copy of Field & Stream Magazine. The black leather 3-seater couch was big enough to seat a few big men, perfect for a Sunday Football extravaganza, or for a guy who had just driven from New York and wanted nothing more than to sleep dreamlessly, as though he were dead. The shower continued to run. I kicked off my shoes and swung my legs up onto the couch, meaning to just relax for a few minutes, let the stress of the road sink down into the cushions. But within a minute, I dozed off.

"Ready to get some ass, baby?" Steve shouted from behind me like we were launching out of a locker room for a big football game or something.

My body shot off the couch.

"Some *ass?*" I asked.

Steve had gone into the shower a homely-looking, quiet gym rat and had somehow reemerged a steroidal lunatic on a mission to get laid. God, I needed to sleep.

"I have a girlfriend," I lied.

"Me, too," he said. "Whiskey shots?"

He stared at me wild-eyed, grinning so widely it seemed he must have extra teeth.

"Did you just do blow in the shower?" I asked, sitting back down to catch my breath.

Steve studied me for an extended moment, perhaps debating if my question was a cut on him or a serious inquiry.

We arrived at the upscale bar with a good buzz already underway. Not long after we got there, Steve pushed several tables aside and started dancing to Journey with a gaggle of tipsy women and shit-faced men. They begged me to join the fracas, but I waved them off and hid on a stool at the corner of the bar area. Steve apparently preferred their company to mine, and that was just fine with me.

A good-looking mountain man in wrangler jeans and a tight-fitting blue and black flannel shirt, 60-ish I guessed, took a seat next to me at the bar after I explained its vacancy by pointing to Steve gyrating on a table.

"Miller," he said with a raised finger to the bartender.

He had the look of a man well-traveled, a man who had seen some of that worldly type shit most of us hadn't. He lit a cigarette slowly, delicately, like it was a lover, and gently placed his matches onto the bar. I wasn't really in the mood for conversation with a stranger, an automatic anxiety booster, but I knew it was coming. All I wanted to do was daydream about Emily and me frolicking down a California beach at sunset, falling into the sand to kiss and admire each other, I had no idea what a beach in California might actually look like, of course, but I had mentally constructed paradise in my spare time the past few years or so and the image in my mind was both vivid and perfect.

"Having fun?" the cowboy lost in Cleveland asked.

Not only did he look like Sam Elliot, but he talked like him, too, a deep, gravelly drawl that made even the most mundane statement seem weighty and profound. I half-expected him to tie back his hair and start kicking everyone's ass like Elliot did in *Roadhouse* with Patrick Swayze.

"Nope. Not at all," I said, again pointing to my new friend, Steve, dry-humping an older woman against a vertical support beam on the dance floor.

"Hurst Ryder," he said and extended his hand for a shake.

Perfect name.

"Tommy Rafferty."

"Beer for your thoughts?" he offered, seeing that my beer was almost gone.

"I guess so, yeah. Thank you."

Hurst signaled the bartender to replace my empty Budweiser with a fresh one. The man clearly wanted to chat and he had bought me a beer. Staying silent was no longer an option.

"I'm traveling," I said, "moving to California. Los Angeles." For some reason, perhaps the Budweisers, I wasn't feeling the need to drop to my hands and knees and start gasping for breath at the prospect of telling a stranger about my ridiculous plan.

"They say it never rains in California."

"Is that right?"

"But it's a downpour of other shit, Tommy," he said with a wise grin.

"You been?"

"In fact, I have. Caught the end of free love, got out before Motley Crue."

I loved insight from men like Hurst, guys who had an understated knowledge about them, who had seen some cool shit but don't seek out an audience to tell the tales. People come to them.

"I was a musician in my past life," he added.

"Rock 'n roll?"

Hurst turned his bar stool to face me, pleased that he might have a decent conversation underway.

"I'm a writer," I blurted out, and now someone aside from Garvey and Mom knew my dark secret. If not for the alcohol, it would have been well past time for an anxiety attack.

"A craft open to inspiration. Groovy. Published?"

"I wrote a movie."

His eyes told me he respected the journey I was undertaking, but that he was also concerned for me. He knew something about LA that I didn't.

"Well? What's it about?" he asked.

"Synchonicity of dreaming. Real life mimics previous night's dreams or nightmares. Something like that, I guess."

Hurst smiled kindly, perhaps aware how uncomfortable it was for me to pitch my work.

"You remind me of Kevin," he said, rubbing the stubble on his cheek in an absent way.

"Kevin?"

Hurst smiled big and said, "Costner. My roommate in California."

I was beginning to look like a Hanson brother (hockey, not boy band) on account of not paying mind to my hygiene like I once did, so this was a pretty heady compliment. I smelled more and more like cheddar Ruffles as the number of days without a shower began to mount.

"Kevin Costner? I remind you of Kevin Costner?"

"Same nougaty center under that hard candy shell. So what's her name?"

"Whose name?"

"The girl in California."

This guy was good.

"I don't know."

"Don't play coy with me, son."

"Emily," I said. "Her name's Emily."

"You've got that lovelorn look all over you," he said. "Kevin couldn't hide that kind of thing, either."

"I've heard Kenickie from *Grease*. But Kevin Costner, wow."

I tucked my hair behind my ears and smoothed my beard like a preening movie star. For a brief moment I forgot I was in my mid-twenties and that I basically had less than two months to sell a script or Dad would disown me.

"He's just a bozo on the bus like the rest of us, Tommy."

"You're telling me Roy McAvoy, *Crash Davis* is just-

"Normal guy."

Hurst grinned wide and ordered us another round with his pointer finger, even though our beers were half full. This guy was too modest to be lying about all this Costner stuff. I wanted more information but didn't want to expose that he had piqued my interest in such shallow things.

"Your pitch, Tommy," he continued "might get you in the room. But don't lose the accent or the work boots. Whatever happens in LA, don't lose sight of who you are or why you're there. That's important."

"Easy to get sidetracked out there, huh?"

"Not for the Costners of the world."

I took a sip of my fresh Budweiser and fantasized about how I could take Hollywood by the balls like Costner had.

"I gotta run," Hurst said, pressing his hands against the edge of the bar and standing in one, smooth motion. "Old lady awaits on the homefront."

"Wait," I said. "Aren't you going to finish your beer?"

Hurst grinned at me, then lifted the bottle from the bar and drained it in one pull. He put the empty bottle back down and rested a big hand on my shoulder.

"It'd be a hell of a lot better," he said, "if this girl of yours had asked you to come."

And then Hurst was gone. As I swiveled my neck to watch him leave, I caught a glimpse of Steve out of the corner of my eye. He was having a conversation with two massive knuckleheads, and even from this distance I could see the talk was not a friendly one. They were pissed, gesticulating in a way that made clear the next step would be blows, and Steve was either too drunk or too stupid—probably both—to back off.

What would a Costner of the world do? I raced over, grabbed Steve by the back of his shirt, and told the knuckleheads that he was hammered, not worth listening to, and further that our night was over and he wouldn't be bothering them anymore. This was enough to squash things, thankfully. We got out of there in one piece and made our way back to Steve's place, where I deposited him in his room and crashed out on the couch, finally able to do all I'd wanted to do in the first place— sleep.

I awoke to sun streaming through the living room windows around seven in the morning. It was early for me to be doing anything but sleeping. I put on the clothes I'd already been wearing for two days and grabbed my toothbrush in the bathroom, and then, having seen enough of Steve to last the rest of my life, hit the door without a goodbye. I stopped for coffee and gas at the mom and pop down the street, then grabbed Route 90 West again and left Cleveland behind, hopefully for good.

As I drove, I thought about Hurst. If not for him, the stop in Cleveland would have been pointless, but I was glad I had the chance meeting with Hurst and told him about my plans, even if they were patchy and likely to end in heartache and disappointment. Something about Hurst's buoyant but realistic attitude regarding my prospects had left me feeling a lot better about things than I had when I'd rolled into town. Most everyone else, when told someone was moving to California to chase their dreams, would respond in one of two extreme ways: either it was the best, most romantic thing they'd ever heard, guaranteed to succeed, or it was the stupidest, most ridiculous thing they'd ever heard, guaranteed to produce nothing but heartache and embarrassment. Hurst, though, split the difference between those two poles: take a mighty hack at the life you want, he seemed to say, but do so with your eyes open, and realize you may end up on your ass in the dirt. Fair enough. I could live with that. I felt pretty good about myself, actually. The ball was rolling, as they say. Win, lose, or draw, I was finally doing something.

Windy City Infamy

The last time I'd been in Chicago was for my cousin Mike's wedding, which took place in the dead of winter. Maybe cousin Mike and his bride would have waited for summer nuptials under different circumstances (or, more likely, would not have gotten married at all), but with twins on the way after a handful of months of dating, Mike had a shotgun in his back. He had to get hitched right then and there, and we all had to accept it and pretend they'd freely made the choice to spend the rest of their lives together. I was eighteen and had long hair, and was uninterested in anything that didn't smell female or taste like beer. I wanted to stay home and throw a party while Mom and Dad went to the wedding, but they were not about to leave me back home to burn their house down.

During the ceremony for cousin Mike at the church, Dad asked if I had remembered to bring my speech for the reception dinner. He gave me a look of mild disgust when I informed him that I hadn't even written a speech, let alone brought it with me. He cracked his neck and pressed his tongue into his cheek, trying his best not to backhand me in front of relatives.

"Tommy," he said, "your mother had this conversation with you twelve hours ago."

Suddenly I remembered: Mom had given me instructions to write a speech the night before at the bar, where the entire family had convened after the rehearsal. That was right about the time that the fourteen rum cocktails I'd slammed were starting to make me nauseous. Everything after that was a blank.

I spent the rest of the ceremony thinking frantically about what I could say that wouldn't embarrass Mike or infuriate my father (further). By the time we got to the reception I still had nothing, and in an effort to jog my brain and calm my nerves, I downed several more rum cocktails on the sly. Predictably, this didn't help. Before I knew it, I was half in the bag, the reception preliminaries were over, and the time had come for me to stand up and give it my best shot.

"Ladies and Gentlemen," I began, looking out at two hundred or so guests with absolutely no idea what I was about to say. "We are gathered here today to celebrate this thing called life." I shook my head and pinched the bridge of my nose, as people chuckled here and there in the crowd. "Cousin Mike is a good guy, as is his bride, Kel-*Karen*, Karen," I continued. "She's something else. And it is only fit that this king should find his princess because they deserve such a thing."

My eyes met Stacy's and I could tell she wanted to help me *so* bad, but there was another part of her that was very much enjoying watching me crash and burn. She, like me, found a humorous lining in pain.

"Chicago is a great town and seeing all of you has been so nice for me and my family to, uh, do that. And it has been good for Mike and Karen, too. I know you are all hungry after that long ceremony at the church there. I know I am, yeah, uh, so let's cut the talk and get down to the food. It's been great sharing this moment with all of you, so congratulations to Mike and Karen Rafferty."

Slow, uneven, quiet applause as people exchanged uncomfortable looks with each other. No doubt this was the worst wedding speech any of them had ever had to endure. My Dad, not surprisingly, was not exchanging looks with anyone. He was too busy boring holes in me with his gaze and wiping the hot beads of sweat streaming down his forehead. For my part, I was too wasted and hungry to be concerned with Dad or his displeasure. I walked clear around his table and took a seat next to some cousins, most of whom I didn't even know.

Up until now, that was the first and only experience I'd had in Chicago, and I was hoping to improve on it as I blew into town and made my way to Adam Steinglass' place.

Adam was a hip Jewish kid no taller than most men's armpits, but he talked a good intellectual game. Just ask him. When he answered the door to his sleek Bucktown apartment, I thought he may have actually shrunk since I saw him last. He was a yarmulke over 5'4" in boots, but his dark rimmed bifocals and black button-down Versace shirt gave him a presence.

"Long way from Chenango Valley, aren't we?" Adam said, holding a full glass of red wine. A native Chicagoan, his accent was strangely English and pompous.

"Ain't that the truth?" I said and shook the light grip of his hand.

Generally speaking, I more than kept pace academically as a college freshman, but then sophomore year came and Organic Chemistry bent me over my lab station and taught me how misplaced my medical school ambitions were. After that I took a new major, Psychology, and barely kept my nostrils above water from then on. I met Adam, an Art History major of the magna cum laude mold, in a junior year Psychology class, where in exchange for a semester's worth of free marijuana he allowed me to ride his coattails all the way to a passing grade.

"Welcome to Chi-town, home of the future World Champion Chicago Cubs," he proclaimed as he grabbed my bag and pointed me to a black marble kitchen countertop that housed an impressive array of liquor and mixers.

Adam and I were known to debate for hours who would win the World Series next, the Cubbies or Red Sox. Neither of had seen our team win in our lifetimes, and may never. Deep down, I knew the Cubs would pull it off first. The Sox had broken my heart too much in 25 years to think otherwise. Anyway, he always talked sports.

"Nice place," I said, helping myself to the Jameson.

"Well thank you, Mr. Tom. I also dig the contrast of black and white and silver."

We went to the living room and sat in two uncomfortable steel bucket chair things. Adam crossed his legs at the knees for effect, and it worked nicely.

"How's the art world?" I asked.

"Ah, you've been keeping tabs on your old buddy?"

"Craigy told me you were working at a gallery."

"I was working at a gallery, this much is true," he said. "Now, I own it."

"Good for you, man."

I raised my glass, and we toasted his success.

"How about we go down to the bar, Tom?" he asked.

"Sure, man. Where did you have in mind?" I asked.

"Joe-Joe's. A *sports* bar," he proclaimed with emphasis like he was unveiling the name of whodunit to a rapt audience.

To Adam, I was the academically challenged stoner, but one who had a gorgeous girlfriend in Emily who always had a couple pretty friends with her. He hitched his wagon to me, if you will. Little did he know I hadn't been with a girl in months myself.

"Sure, let's finish these up and I'll rinse off and change up," I said.

"Brilliant. *Brilliant.*"

As I lathered my body in blue liquid soap, paying special attention to the area I had sat on all day, I realized Adam had not asked any questions about me or my life. I had asked about him and the gallery, even toasted his success, but there was no talk about why I was in Chicago or where I was heading. Zilch. Which in retrospect should have

35

made me suspicious. But at that moment, other than making quick note of his utter lack of curiosity about me and what I was doing, I didn't think much of it.

Meeting a woman at a bar is a crapshoot. You never get the full picture of her. You're only getting the best she has to offer. Why else would she be there, to showcase the crusty side of her? That side of things usually waits until the morning when she awakes with no make-up, morning breath, and a really spooky comment about how something about the previous night felt 'different' or 'special'.

Emily was probably the only girl I knew who didn't blatantly showcase herself. She didn't walk into a bar like a model on a runway, casting faraway eyes and stepping to the beat of the house music. Fact is, she didn't need to. She was damn near perfect and she knew it. Maybe, if my intention was to win Emily back, I owed her my fidelity in advance. Maybe I was being selfish. But maybe, just maybe, Emily was having barbarian sex that very moment with her new boyfriend. A lot of 'maybe's" to process.

Maybe I should be open to other women and enjoy myself.

God bless alcohol.

The woman I met at the bar, who had the unlikely name of Ambrosia, would spare me the aforementioned morning hassle, I thought, so I went forward with the small talk after she floated into my vicinity. She was clearly no stranger to a commitment-free roll in the hay.

"You have a girlfriend?" she said from below my nose, looking up at me with a hand on my belt.

"No girlfriend here," I said uncomfortably as if a cop was patting me down and I had a joint stuffed in my sock. Truth was, I didn't have a girlfriend. Despite the cocktails coursing my mind, I registered in that moment that it felt like a lie to say that I didn't have a girlfriend.

Ambrosia knew I was a ship in the night, and would be back at sea tomorrow, yet she still remained close by at Joe-Joe's pressing herself against my arms and chest. Adam was more than happy with Ambrosia's horny friend who had a mass of tomato-red hair that looked as though it was running mad from her skull. I thought of Raggedy Anne, but nicer clothes and holding Parliament Lights.

"We could head back to my place for a nightcap," Adam interjected to the group. "What do you think, Mr. Tom?"

"Sounds good to me. Ladies?" I asked.

"You won't kidnap me to California, will you?" Ambrosia said, making clear her hope was that I would.

"I'll get the cab," Adam blurted, disappearing into the crowd quickly. Ambrosia, Flame Top and I slammed the remainder of our cocktails and rose to catch up with him.

Eleven minutes later, Ambrosia and I barged into my bedroom. I shot my pants to my ankles like a 5-year-old running to a bubble bath.

In the break of action, I heard Adam giggle outside the door. Ambrosia was taking a break in the bathroom and must've been busy ruffling her hair or something, so she didn't hear him. I stepped through the legs of my jeans, tossed my hair back and went outside to see if Adam was making any progress with Flame Top and why he was standing outside my door like a pervert.

"So why did Tom go crazy?" I heard Flame Top ask Adam from where they were snuggling on the couch.

"Craigy, our friend in New York, said Tom has lost his shit finally with Emily and all."

I debated whether to turn the corner into the living room or stay in the weeds and hear the horrible truth. I froze and listened.

"Who's Emily?" Flame Top asked Adam.

"Tom's college girlfriend. Prettier than a Monet."

"And?"

"He's delusional. She moved on long ago. Took his sanity with her."

Emily never liked you, Adam, how would you know how she feels?

"Sad," Flame Top submitted by way of analysis.

"It is, isn't it? When people think of Tom now, they don't think of the carefree go-getter anymore with the 1,000-watt smile. They see his remains, what's been salvaged from the Emily fiasco."

"Did she cheat on him?"

"Relentlessly. God yes, she did."

"Did he know?"

"He knew about one or two." Adam said and I pictured the smug grin of a man backstabbing his friend to impress a woman. I wanted a refund for all the pot I gave him in college.

"You're different," Flame Top said to Adam before I heard a loud smacking sound from the meeting of their stupid lips.

"Really?" Adam asked in nauseating baby talk.

"I mean it."

Adam probably bought it. Asshole.

I was pissed. I needed my laptop and I needed Ambrosia to vacate the premises, immediately.

I tiptoed back into "my" bedroom to find Ambrosia passed out on top of the sheets. It was time to bang out some words, but not before I raced into the bathroom to chug water out of the faucet and pop a Lorazepam to hedge the looming hangover.

I wrote best when I wanted to place the world on the floor and jump on it and grind the bastard into the pavement. Teeth grinding fits of anger could bring out a frantic writing frenzy more than any other emotion. When I was done exercising the anger demons, I usually had a large weight lifted from my chest and placed into my journal, which was really just a Microsoft Word document in a well-hidden folder on my laptop. I'd then use the words and stories from my journal and try to apply it to my script. I pulled out my laptop and began to stomp the world.

Only a few minutes later, just as I was getting going, Ambrosia broke the spell with a loud fart.

"Excuse me," she muttered with a giggle in her sleep, eyes still closed, and rolled her ass away from me.

Emily farted once, I think, but I didn't actually hear it and we were driving by the ocean at low tide so I wasn't totally sure about it. I shot a smile in the direction of Ambrosia and pulled my t-shirt up to my nose with a giggle, praying aloud that I didn't catch a funky draft coming from her direction. I returned to my journal with less hostility.

But it was no good. I was too preoccupied with Ambrosia to concentrate on writing anymore. And I was too dead tired from traveling and thinking. Plus the Lorazepam was doing its job. All the mojo that had come on so suddenly had just as suddenly abandoned me, so I closed my laptop and crawled into bed with Ambrosia.

The next morning, the girls were gone without a trace when I awoke. I felt bad I hadn't had a chance to say good-bye, but also glad that I'd been spared the awkward morning-after dance of regret and shame. We'd both had an itch and we'd both been drunk enough to scratch it. Better for everyone to avoid a needless postmortem in the light of day.

Adam warned me that his roommate, Alfie, was terribly anal (as if Adam himself was not) so we had to clean up really well in the room that I had contaminated with sex. Adam, of course, only knew we had sex because he stuck his nose into my business the night before with his nosy little recon mission. After about a half hour we had finished cleaning the bedroom and his apartment, and my mind could not get over Adam's words about his friend – me - to this girl he hardly knew. Maybe our definitions of "friend" were changing, or growing apart. I suppose we were now a few years out of college where people can start to change.

Adam offered to pay for a Bloody Mary and plate of scrambled eggs at the greasy spoon joint around the way.

"No, I think I'll get going, Adam."

"You sure?"

"Yeah, I'm sure. But thank you."

"It's just a bed," he said with his hands raised. "Least I can do."

"Hey, good luck with the art gallery and all," I said.

"Thanks, Tom. And good luck with all your, you know, stuff."

I couldn't let it go.

"What stuff would that be, Adam?" I asked.

I turned to face him and he got nervous, but I would never hurt him physically. I just wanted to see, hear, and feel his answer with my undivided attention.

I continued, "I haven't said a word about where I'm going, what I'm doing, or why. So... what, exactly, are you wishing me luck with?"

Not even Adam's big brain could help him with this one. He was stuck and I could tell he felt regret. At least he felt regret, though.

"Sorry, man," he said finally. "Craigy told me what's going on. He's worried about you, is all."

I studied his eyes for an extended beat, figuring out where to take this conversation.

"I'm not the mess you two think I am," I said.

"Opinions vary," Adam said, and I managed a tight smile. He could do that.

"We love you, Tommy," he continued, "You have more balls than Craigy and I combined".

I can't lie and say that wasn't nice to hear.

We hugged briefly, awkwardly given the conversation that had just unfolded, and I hoisted my bag from the floor.

Leaving Chicago, I found myself contemplating Ambrosia and the pre-fart era of our relationship. Maybe I'd been right in thinking that if I wanted to be with Emily, I had to change the behaviors and indulgences that had ended things in the first place. Still, I felt fine about it. I wasn't concerned that Emily would hate me even more for having a fling with a random girl from a bar. Maybe this wasn't enough to erase the speech at cousin Mike's wedding that went down in infamy, but my Chicago legacy had improved, if only marginally.

Hotdogs to Go

I could hardly believe I was driving back to Sun Valley, Idaho. It was like a *Twilight Zone* episode from the 80s, a sort of out of body, spooky experience.

The drive from Chicago to Sun Valley, Idaho is hard on a guy on the run, a guy with all his 'stuff,' as Adam said. For the emotionally stable type, the road is wide-open and features just enough attractions along the way to keep one from introspection-induced insanity. The Mississippi and Missouri rivers. Badlands National Park. Mount Rushmore. Yellowstone and the Grand Tetons. But for someone like me, there's too much time in between natural wonders, too much opportunity to get in trouble inside my own head. The good feelings of Chicago had long since dwindled, and the Lorazepam was no match for the vast emptiness of the Great Plains. I cycled through all the feelings, none of them good, until anger finally overtook me somewhere in the Badlands. I swerved off the highway into a rest area, staggered out of the truck, and started climbing upward by foot in my shorts and bare feet, no water, no trail to follow, no real sense of what I was doing or why.

After a while I reached an outcropping with a view of all that desolation. Rocks and sky for as far as the eye could see. I might have been the only man alive, and honestly, in that moment, that would have been fine by me. I recognized that I was having some kind of internal reckoning, experiencing a personal inflection point. I had to get through this, whatever it was, by myself, without the aid of my mother or friends or Lorazepam, and when it was over, I would know what was what. I would either continue west, get to California, and pursue my dreams, or I would tuck tail and head back east. But either way I was about to get closer to who I am, and maybe even what life intended for me. There would be no more waffling. There would be no more indecision. This was an either/or moment, a genuine binary, and I was in the midst of it, right there at the edge of the world.

The endless outlay of rocks and dust seemed to know who I was and understand my pain. They embraced me. I was brought to my knees, quite literally. With no drink or woman or old friend to insulate me from myself, I was consumed in the realest emotions I had ever felt.

Suddenly, without even really making the decision to do so, I started screaming for the entire world to hear. At first, I was shocked at the sound of my own voice. After 20 minutes of tossing curses and threats into the wind, I lay flat on my stomach and rested my forehead against the rock's surface, exhausted and borne out.

I stayed on that rock in the Badlands for almost two full hours, the anger receding slowly, a process that felt similar, I imagined, to what it would be like to bleed out. Occasionally a family drove by in a station wagon or camper, just a dot on the horizon at first, then taking shape as they slowly drew closer until I could see faces looking out at me through the windows as they passed. They'd look at me with trepidation, suspicious of my placement in the middle of nowhere without a camera or driving map flapping in the wind. No, I wasn't out of gas. I was poking the world in the chest and standing some ground for once. I refused to take a Lorazepam. If my heart jumped out of my chest, so be it. On that rock I wore nothing but a pair of shorts and sunglasses. No shoes, no shirt, no needless baggage on my body or soul. Tarzan had nothing on me.

When I finally, slowly pulled myself to my feet and climbed back down to my truck, it was very clear that something had changed, though I wouldn't have been able to explain what exactly. As I drove further west, the sweat of my back clung to the cloth seat cushion and the images of a manageable world clung to my mind, soft and clear, and I drove through them. I thought about the miles I had driven and the road in front of me, which I would take in without pills numbing my mind. No more drugs.

****

My newfound determination to eschew old habits would, of course, not go unchallenged. After all, old friends meant old ways, a fact about which I was entirely mindful as I pulled my truck into the parking lot of The Basement Pub in my post-college stomping grounds of Sun Valley.

My college buddies Ryan and Damian had built the place from the ground up, and were now operating at a healthy profit. I knocked on the door to the pub and waited a few short moments until Damian answered, larger than life as always, a big smile on his face.

Built like the tough farmer he was groomed to be, Damian is an imposing figure, but has always been a humble guy who gravitated to a nice conversation and gentle whiskey pour. The son of a northern California almond farmer, Damian spent his summers waking at the crack of dawn to lend a hand to his father and grandfather, learning the family business in the assumption that he would inherit it. I suppose there's still time for him to take the reins of the farm, but I doubt it will ever happen. He prefers the clean air of the mountains, being a loner in his townhouse outside town and the unlimited access to a wonderful liquor cabinet – his bar he owns. Damian likes his drink, let's say, as evidenced by the fact that he had answered the door with a bottle of Tullamore Dew as a welcoming present. It was 11 o'clock in the morning.

"Before you say anything, follow me, Raff," Damian said. "I've got a surprise for you." He put one heavy arm around my shoulders and guided me into the darkness of the pub. I stayed quiet and walked with him, equal parts anxious and excited.

My mind raced with memories of helping them put the bar together, hanging old family pictures, wrestling with the stereo system wiring, smearing the wood beams with noxious cherry stain, installing that heavier-than-all-hell shuffle board table, and a slew of other tasks we somehow managed to pull off despite the fact that none of us really had any training or skill as a builder.

I followed Damian around the corner of the bar into the pool table room, where the surprise awaited: Above the pool table on the back wall, my college baseball jersey had been pressed and framed in a beautiful glass case. I had no clue how they got it from the University, but there it was. As we approached the glass case, I could see that inside the case was the original copy of a note I had slipped under the door for Ryan and Damian the morning I had left Sun Valley for Boston. It was a quote from a movie I'd long since forgotten, but the quote itself would now forever be etched in my mind:

If you got yourself two or three good pals, then you got yourself a tribe.

And there ain't nothing stronger than that.

Your PAL,

Tommy Rafferty

"Welcome back, pal," Damian said, and we pulled up barstools while he poured whiskey.

He probably didn't see me wipe a tear from my eye with my cocktail napkin, but I didn't really care if he did or not. I was fully committed now to the complete overhaul of my life, and it scared me to death. I was, in other words, fragile. Fragile, but feeling almost human, aware of a world outside my head, for the first time in a while.

The door whipped open as I blotted my eyes and there stood Ryan "Ryno" Dennehy, the one man I will call if I ever get thrown in jail for more than ten years and need some help with the escape. Ryan was

47

also from a Boston suburb and ended up in upstate New York for college with me. Salt of the earth.

"Raff!" Ryan darted towards me, arms held wide.

"Ryno," I said and rose from my barstool to accept his hug.

"Let's get out of this dump. Schooners at Grumpy's?" Ryan asked as he measured my conditional approval.

Grumpy's Grill was the epicenter of my debasement four years ago. The sound of its name sent chills through my body. I could almost taste the next day's hangover on my tongue as I waited for Damian to weigh in on the idea.

"Perfect," said Damian, but I'm pretty sure I heard a slight lack of conviction.

To my surprise, as we got to talking and drinking, I learned that Damian and Ryan had become full-fledged adults in the relatively short amount of time that I had left Sun Valley for Boston. Maybe it was owning the Pub that shook them into a responsible state. Whatever it was, they were doing well, something was different, and I felt, well, immature. They were so reformed, shall we say, from the partying we subjected ourselves to in a horrible two-year spell of nightly intoxication, that we actually started toying with the idea of me moving back to Sun Valley. They'd changed their lives, and I was ready to change mine. They both had purchased homes, had plenty of space for me to crash, a job to help me get started – all that.

In the midst of an ever-deepening alcoholic haze, it all made sense: forget California, forget screenwriting, forget Emily. I'd just drop anchor here again, help Ryan and Damian run the bar, get myself sorted out, and determine what my life would look like going forward as a real, full-fledged, non-sedative-dependent grown up.

We dipped in and out of a few bars to end the night, running into some familiar faces as we went. Something felt so right about the three of us raging unapologetically through a rustic Western town so far from city life. Things got grey and then black, and some time later I woke up on a couch. I wasn't sure if this was Damian's place, or Ryan's, but I was sure that I'd had way too much to drink, and now, all of a sudden, the notion of staying on in Sun Valley seemed exactly as absurd as it was.

I had managed to blackout the majority of the night on account of whiskey shots, as did Ryan and Damian, who were still sleeping in different locations in the house. We had landed somehow at Damian's place, as far as I could gather from the family photos on the walls. I felt like I had licked an ashtray, puked up all nutrients in my body, and stuck a few thumbtacks in my temples.

I stumbled slowly into the bathroom to check my face for the enormous bruises and cuts that would explain my unbearable headache, but was oddly dismayed to find that everything was more or less in place. Other than a pronounced alcoholic puffiness, there was nothing wrong with my face. No big cowboy had rearranged my features. All my teeth were where they belonged, and my knuckles were free of damage.

As I stood there wondering how I could have gotten it in my head that staying in Sun Valley was a good idea, I heard rustling in a room nearby. A few seconds later, Damian came into the bathroom wearing nothing but boxers and a confused, pained look on his face.

"You have yellow mustard all over your face," I informed him.

I had barely finished my sentence when, without warning or preamble, Damian leaned over the toilet and half-digested hot dogs erupted out of his mouth. I tried not to look, tried not to *smell,* tried my best to find a happy place in my head, but it was no use. I put my hands on the sink, leaned down, and discovered in the most violent, unpleasant fashion that Damian wasn't the only one who'd indulged in an excessive number of meat tubes the previous evening.

Damian patted me on the back as I continued to heave and convulse. "Frozen hot dogs when we got home," he said, wiping at his lips and cheeks with the back of his hand.

Finally emptied of the offending nitrites, I leaned against the wall and sank to the floor. "Did we have fun last night?" I asked.

"I was hoping you could tell me," Damian said.

I thought about my question for a moment, partly because my brain was lost in fog, and partly because I wasn't sure if the whole experience, from last night until now, could ever be called "fun" once one has the benefit of hindsight.

This sort of self-abuse had, not too long ago, seemed like the best time going. But that had also been a period of my life when I had nothing weighty or consequential on my mind. A time when twenty-five seemed impossibly old, an age we'd never reach. A time before panic attacks and countless nights spent staring at the ceiling, wondering what the hell I was doing, or what the hell I would do going forward. A time when Jackie was still alive and well on the Cape.

"This morning sucks, I know that much," I told him.

Damian half-coughed, half-gagged into his fist. "That," he said, managing a smile, "may be the understatement of the year."

We slowly straightened our backs and looked at each other, our eyes bloodshot and rheumy.

"We'd go right back to this nonsense every night if I stayed," I said.

"Ryan and I would drink all the profits."

"I'd help."

"Everyone would get fat. Lose their teeth."

Damian grinned in a way that told me he was happy to see me, but he and Ryan had their lives here, and I didn't fit into that equation, either for them, or for myself. It was time to keep rolling west, and there was absolutely no arguing that fact. If I left Sun Valley, this time on my terms and with a clearer mind, I was taking something back that was rightfully mine – my will. Lost evenings, regurgitated hot dogs—if I hadn't known before, now I knew without a doubt that I had to strongly consider putting this collegiate buffoonery to rest. And Damian wanted to do it, too, had to do it, just like I did.

As I got back on the road, the reflexive, knee-jerk urge to pop a couple pills and quiet the barking in my head came over me. That was always the move, the easy fix, with a hangover like this. A headache and upset stomach were easy enough to deal with, but the truly fearful part of an epic hangover, for me, was about anxiety, a baseline of existential ennui running in the background and reminding me of everything I'd failed at, everything I hadn't accomplished, everything that scared and saddened me. At their worst, these hangovers were like a house of horrors. But I realized, as I considered whether or not to take the Lorazepam, that now the urge felt more like a habitual inclination and less like an absolute necessity to keep from losing my mind. I had a choice to make: I could keep leaning on the drugs, or I could deal with the shit I'd been avoiding all this time, meet it head-on. I swore off the drugs since that rock in the Badlands, but apparently, subconsciously or not, had not thrown out the bottle. It was time to face the music, my soundtrack, the good and bad cuts alike, with a clearer head and a raw, open-to-anything soul.

Before I could think a second longer and talk myself out of it, I grabbed the pill bottle from the center console and tossed it out the window.

The Lorazepam jumped down the road in my rearview mirror.

And then, for the next thirteen hours, I oscillated between confidence and cowardice, optimism and a crushing sense of certain doom. One moment I was certain I would conquer Hollywood. The next, equally certain I'd die penniless and insane in a cardboard lean-to on Skid Row. I probably sucked my thumb to get through the mad abstraction of thoughts.

After a while, even the moments of optimism became exhausting. I nearly succumbed to the heat, as did my truck, losing its ability to accelerate up the smallest of hills coming through Death Valley. As my wheels spun me closer to my destination, I had a strange, nonsensical, yet nonetheless powerful conviction that California wouldn't accept me. As though California had a consciousness, and made active decisions about who it would and would not admit. Maybe I wasn't good enough. Maybe

I was a fool for trying to infiltrate the entertainment business. I didn't know who the fucking genius was that decided to ditch the Lorazepam, but I had a hard time believing *I* could be so stupid. I was damn near hyperventilating myself into unconsciousness as I passed the first highway sign that warned Hollywood was approaching.

And when I finally did reach Hollywood, I was certain that I had made a wrong turn. The place was public urinal filthy, populated by an assortment of freaks and junkies unlike anything I'd seen before in my life. Maybe I'd gone to Hollywood, Nevada by mistake? No way this could be what I'd left Boston behind for.

But here I was. As I sat at a red light, wondering where I might be headed and what would happen to me when I got there, a 6'4" man in stiletto heels approached, yelling at me about his need for spare change. I usually gave a nickel or a quarter to the homeless, but this guy on Sunset was too much to take. I rolled up my window as he approached my truck with hands extended. I had never seen a man in heels, let alone a big, Rick James-ish, bearded street hooker (little did I know that he was hardly the most unusual sight on the Sunset Strip, a fact I would become well-acquainted with over the next few months). I thought to tell him he'd likely have more luck if he didn't storm towards drivers' windows out of the scarier-than-all-hell blue, but I wasn't about to roll the window back down to facilitate a conversation. Instead I employed the same strategy people have used from time immemorial when dealing with the homeless: I pretended he wasn't there. For what seemed like hours I stared straight ahead, silently cursing what had to be the slowest traffic light in creation, until after eternity and five minutes the light finally changed, and I sped safely away.

Touching Down

I cruised up Santa Monica Boulevard in search of an apartment suitable for a man down to $509.12 and in need of gas and a meal. This place was not at all what I'd thought it would be, but I was here and that was that. Once again, there was no use fighting reality. The town must have a heart somewhere and I imagined, or at least hoped, or at least was trying to convince myself, that I was just the guy to find it.

After filling the gas tank and devouring a meal of tacos and tortilla chips, I would need to shave. And after I shaved, I would need to do laundry and clip my toenails and fingernails. After that, I needed to find a literary agent and sell my script in the next few weeks for a million dollars, or else Dad would likely come kick my ass and drag me home.

A yellow neon sign reading VACANCY: MONTH-TO-MONTH caught my eye, as did the drug dealers plying their wares in the street below the sign. I waited out a line of oncoming traffic, then pulled left into the parking lot, double-checking as I got out of the truck to make sure the doors were all locked. Swinging open the glass door to the main office in front of the motel, I still felt dizzy and tired after wrestling my mind for so long through the desert.

"Welcome to Rosa's," a leather-faced Mexican lady with greasy, waist-length black hair said as I entered.

I stretched, reaching my hands toward the ceiling.

"Hello there, R-r-r-Rosa," I said with a charming roll of the tongue.

"Not Rosa. Emilia. Rosa dead," she said, somewhat matter-of-factly given the topic. "You need room, no?"

"I do, yes. How much per month, sweetheart?"

"Five-hundred dollars."

"C'mon, that's the worst room you have?" I asked, offering what I hoped was a charming smile.

"We have one other room, pero muy poquito, uh, very small. Four hundred. Smells like cats and cigarillos, no?"

I hated cats.

"Three fifty," I said.

She just stared. "Cuatrocientos," she said.

I had no idea what this meant, so I reached for my wallet, pulled out three hundred-dollar bills and a fifty, and placed them on the counter. She eyed the money without moving to take it, then looked at me again.

"Fifty more," she said.

"Three-fifty," I said, jabbing at the money already on the counter with my index finger. "Take it or leave it."

She paused a moment longer, did a calculus in her head regarding how likely it was that someone else would come in and rent her shitbox room for full price, then finally nodded. "Your roommate is Katherine," she said.

"Roommate?" I asked. I reached over to take the bills back, but she was too quick for me, snatching the money up and putting it safely in the register.

"Si. No problemo. Very sweet. Very good. Movie director. *Very* good."

A movie director roommate in a cheap apartment sounded brilliant, but it also sounded like a solid justification to further negotiate the price down. Of course, I had considerably less bargaining leverage with my money already in the register rather than my wallet. Still, I intended to try.

"We sleep in the same room?" I asked.

"Big room. Very big room," she said and stretched out her arms to her sides.

"Ooh, no good, Emilia. Different bathrooms?"

"No. Same bathroom."

"No good. I use my own bathroom," I said with a pained look, rubbing my stomach as if I had an imminent bowel issue.

Emilia had seen my game before and flipped me a copy of Westside Rentals, a booklet of all current rentals in the area. I raced through the booklet and it was plain to see that I was priced out of anything remotely livable. Nothing under $600/month within twenty miles of Hollywood. Even if there had been, I was too beaten to investigate, anyway.

"One month. Four hundred," I said.

Rosa won.

Emilia didn't really do the room the justice it deserved. It was very cozy. That is, if you've been sleeping on cracked pavement in Alaska for the past month. It was not just a cat piss infested den, as Emilia suggested. It was more than that. It was the kind of a place where desperate, drunken old men bring twenty-dollar hookers for the night. The kind of place where junkies stack up their afternoons overdosing in the bathroom and using the carpet as an ashtray. That kind of place.

"You like, no?" Emilia asked as I stood in the doorway of my new pad, afraid to cross the threshold.

"No," I said, too shocked to even consider lying.

We stepped inside to get a better look at the place. The plastic blinds, or the broken, seemingly gnawed-upon remnants of what had once presumably been plastic blinds, were permanently open. I imagined the drawstrings had been yanked off by a kidnapping victim trying to escape a Hannibal Lecter-type.

"Your bed there," Emilia said with a finger pointed at a pencil thin egg crate mattress atop a flimsy, rusted box spring on the floor in the corner of the living room.

"No bed frame?"

"No need."

I was broke, and it was either stay here or head back to Boston, tail firmly tucked.

"It's fine. Thank you, Emilia."

"You need me, I downstairs."

Emilia scooted away before I could decide that this wasn't such a good idea. For all I knew, this was a nice place where Emilia came from and I didn't want to hurt her feelings, so I let her go and decided one month couldn't be too much to handle. I went down to the car and grabbed my laptop, golf clubs and oversized L.L. Bean travel bag full of my clothes.

The alleged movie director roommate, allegedly named Katherine, was not there to stake her claim to certain areas of the apartment, but I did my best not to invade spaces that already seemed occupied. I could only hope that Emilia had informed Katherine that her apartment could at any time, and without notice, become double-occupancy and co-ed. Must have? Insane, nonetheless.

I was starving still, even after the tacos, but too tired to do anything but make my bed and sleep, despite the fact that it was only six o'clock at night. Luckily, I'd thought to pack my own bed sheets, so wouldn't have to sleep on the bare eggcrate, which no doubt harbored any number of things that would be happy to make their home on or in my body.

Before crawling into bed, I taped a note on the door for Katherine that read:

Dear Katherine,

I am your new roommate. Emilia let me in. I am a male, but I am nice.

Look forward to meeting you!

Tommy Rafferty.

I half expected to wake up at some point in the night to Katherine shouting threats my way, an iron skillet in hand. But I was too tired, finally, to worry about what tomorrow would bring, so I dozed off in my new home, asleep almost before my head hit the filthy pillow.

I woke disoriented, looked around the room, and saw the living room clock read 11:23. Day or night? Who knew? I lay on my back, took a deep breath, and sank into a fantasy about a Dunkin Donuts French Vanilla the size of a mop bucket.

"Hello there, roomie," a disembodied voice said from the tiny kitchen.

I shot up in bed and yanked my hands out of my warm boxers.

"Hello?" I replied, reaching for my glasses on the nasty carpet next to the bed.

"You have a message here."

"Huh? Are you, um, um—"

"I wrote it down for you."

I stood up and spied a petite brunette at the dinged-up table. She slouched in her chair, facing the doorway, like she had been there for hours waiting for me to wake up.

"You answered my phone?"

"Well, I guess. I heard it go off and—"

"Yeah, cool, thanks. No big deal. You must be, uh, Kather . . ."

"Katie. Katie Ketchup," she said.

"Tommy Poupon, how are you?" I said.

I moved to offer my hand.

"Cute."

"Sorry. Tommy Rafferty."

Katie finally stood and slung her purse around one tanned shoulder. Her cargo pants and ruffled off-the-shoulder blouse signified a touch of wealth. I wondered if she was slumming it in this dump with vagabonds like me for cinematic inspiration.

"Okay then. Don't flush the toilet, Tommy Rafferty."

"Like, at all?"

Katie was in a hurry all of a sudden, headed toward the door. Maybe she had been waiting for me to come to just to warn me about the toilet situation.

"It overflows all over the entire apartment," she continued.

"So what do we do when…"

"Just don't flush the toilet," she said. She looked at me, one hand on the door handle, and shrugged.

I looked down at my bare feet, thinking about how only a moment before I'd thought the floor was merely filthy; now I knew it was likely covered in a living, breathing health hazard. Katie bolted out the door with a wave over her shoulder, and I hit the moldy shower and spent extra time scrubbing the soles of my feet.

Before I headed out for breakfast in Hollywood, I called home, intending to tell my parents that I was alive and more or less well. They weren't home, so I left a corny, upbeat message on their answering machine: what I saw on my trip, who I'd spent time with, where I was now living (with some of the more gruesome details left out), and what my short-term plan would be. Dad would be happy, no doubt, that I didn't mention Emily's name. My poor mom, though. I knew Garvey would be stopping by to visit them to talk about me so I asked my parents to please to tell Garvey that I said hello and that I would call him soon, as soon as I got my cell plan changed so I wouldn't run up roaming charges. And then I realized there wasn't much else to say, so I hung up and stepped out the door.

Hollywood, baby.

I walked the streets for a solid two hours with a cup of coffee in hand, step over step to nowhere in particular. The sun beat down and I got cranky sooner than I had hoped. I started to make those judgmental observations that insecure people can make about others, especially those of a stranger in an entirely strange land. For example, in Boston, you showed off to the neighbors by scoring rafter seats to a Bruins playoff game. In Hollywood, people drove hundred-thousand-dollar Hummers that could withstand a missile attack just to go to the grocery store. And they all seemed to park directly in front of the store, retrieving the young ones from their baby seats, putting on their dark sunglasses, lowering their "I might be famous" baseball caps, and walking into the place like they owned it. They were all over the place, these false-positives, wannabe famous people who weren't famous at all but played it all cloak-and-dagger like they were. It took me all of this single morning of non-Pitts and non-Annistons in Von Dutch hats to lose interest in seeing the real versions of them. From Fairfax to La Brea, from Melrose to Sunset, this place was giving me the creeps.

I finished lunch at a place called Dublin's on Sunset Boulevard, the strangest, saddest excuse for an Irish pub I'd ever seen up to that point in my life. I imagined that the Murphys and Sullivans back in

Boston would be both amused and horrified by the young man behind the bar lip-synching Madonna as he dabbed a stain on his blouse with seltzer. I'd gone to Dublin's hoping for a little taste of home, and instead felt farther from Boston than I ever had before.

Fore!

Back home I knew most every golf course from Boston down to the Cape. There was Widow's Walk in nearby Scituate, a really tough track that I loved on the waterfront. There was Duxbury Yacht Club, a beautifully maintained course, the exclusivity of which forced us non-members to sneak on, before they inevitably found us chugging beers and kicked us out for the umpteenth time. Then there was New Seabury Country Club down the Cape, a tough course with a lot of cool old-timers. Or I would cruise through a round at a public course like Braintree Muni, North Hill, Waverly, Pinehills, or Frank Wright and come out completely satisfied. It was nice to know which courses to play, at what time of year, on which day of the week, and at what price. I knew nothing of L.A. golf but I was excited to get out.

On the half hour drive south to Alondra Country Club in Redondo Beach, California started to look a lot more like what I'd seen on television and in magazines. I caught the sweet smell of the ocean as I got further from Hollywood, and there were a lot fewer junkies distracting from the canvas. Even though I still had no money and hadn't yet done a thing to get my screenwriting career started, just getting to the golf course and breathing the clean air inspired a sunny optimism I hadn't felt in a long time. I could see, suddenly, why people loved Southern California. Golf weather all year? What could possibly be better than that?

I heard the starter at Alondra call my name over the intercom system and scurried up from the practice green to meet my playing partners and get things started. To my delight, the course was not crowded and I was given only one partner for the round. Fewer people generally meant a better pace of play. That was the upside. The downside was that I could tell, before we even shook hands and exchanged pleasantries, that my one partner was a world-class douchebag. His name was Eric Dobbs, a thirty-year-old pediatrician from Manhattan Beach, the highest of high rent districts around here, I'd learn.

"Bring your A-game?", he asked as I teed up my striped Titleist marked RANGE to begin the round.

For whatever reason, golf is a game that inspires these kinds of corny one-liners, and some players carry a few more than others. Some, like this Dobbs, carry too many.

"If I make contact, I'm off to a good start," I replied, and I meant it.

I checked my grip and the alignment of my flip-flops in relation to the ball before bringing the club head back and uncorking a home run swing that carried the ball a good 250 yards up the right side of the fairway.

"We've got a sandbagger," Dobbs said.

As well as featuring corny one-liners, golf is the kind of sport that inspires 14-handicap weekend warriors to dress like they're card-carrying

PGA tour players—assuming they have the money to be able to afford it. Dobbs had the money. His beige slacks were spotless and neatly pressed, probably by a Mexican woman he paid five bucks an hour under the table. His black Nike shirt fit his drooping shoulders nicely and the white swoosh on his chest looked very Tiger-ish. The matching Foot-Joy glove, socks and spikes Dobbs wore were whiter and brighter than Elmer's glue.

He stepped up to the tee box and leveled the head of a new Cleveland driver at a fresh-out-the-box Titleist ProV1. The illusion of a skilled golfer was seamless, the runway seemingly clear for an under-par round, until he took that first hack and nearly twirled himself into the ground with a Sammy Sosa whiff. The ball fell off the tee like a meatball flopping off the side of a plate. Not good.

"Mulligan?" he asked, clutching his lower back and looking around for witnesses.

Even though it was one o'clock in the afternoon, I really didn't care if this douche-bag took a breakfast ball, as long as he hurried up.

"Have at it," I said.

Sadly, hurrying up did not seem to be in the cards, because Dobbs proved the first time was no fluke by missing the ball again, despite the fact that he took a little off his swing. On the third attempt he finally made contact, but very little of it, worm-burning the ball barely past the ladies tees.

"I haven't played in ages," he said.

I lit a smoke, and we were off.

Dobbs knew every intricacy of the golf swing and the original pioneer behind each particular nuance. *Byron says do this. Harmon says do that.* Dobbs passed this knowledge onto me as if I'd asked for it, usually when I was in the middle of my backswing or lining up a tricky par putt with seven feet of break. Other times he'd wait until I was looking for my ball in the woods while he stood a long enough distance away to plausibly avoid helping without *looking like* he was avoiding helping. For all of his supposed knowledge of the game, and for all the time he clearly spent reading and thinking about it, Dobbs seemed completely unaware of its real purpose, at least for duffers like us. It's supposed to be about making friends and having a few laughs, maybe even throwing together a decent score on the card at the end of the day.

"The putting stroke is more pendulum than a two-part motion. It's flow, it's all flow of the wrists," Dobbs said as he stood above his third putt to salvage triple bogey on the eighth hole.

Just hit the poor ball, Tiger.

The putt miraculously dropped into the cup and Dobbs' goofy smile broadcast that he thought he was really onto something with that whole pendulum theory.

We hit our drives off the ninth tee box and I tuned out more golf theory as we headed up the fairway to hit our second shots. For the first time all day, we were both in the fairway off the tee and Dobbs was quick to credit my blast to his advice on swing tempo.

"You see, Tommy? It works," he said.

We reached Dobbs' ball first and I rested my bag under my forearms as I watched him take his customary five to ten practice swings.

67

I was playing alone because I didn't have any friends, but by now I knew Dobbs was playing alone because he'd burned every golf partner he had ever encountered. Not even his mother wanted to listen to his commentary on the sport or wait for him to catch up.

After his final practice swing, he threw a piece of grass above his head to judge the wind, as if his shot would rise to a height where wind might affect it. It seemed, finally, mercifully, as though the time had come when he would hit the goddamn ball. But instead, that was the moment he got shot by a sniper.

Until that moment I had never actually seen a golfer get hit with a golf ball. A golf cart I was driving got nailed head-on once, but the windshield spared me any injury. Garvey got hit in the ankle once, but I didn't see it happen from the other side of the fairway and no one was hurt. He just swatted at his ankle and laughed.

In this case, it's like realtors say: location, location, location.

Tee shot, 235 yards, dropping down out of the sky and hitting Dobbs squarely in the cubes. It's unthinkable bad luck. And I'm no statistician, but the actual odds of it happening had to be astronomical, and yet, there we were: Dobbs fell to the ground like he'd been shot point-blank with a .45, eyes somehow both bulging and crossed. And yeah, I laughed—both because it was funny, and because if I could have chosen the first person I'd see catch a golf ball in the nuts, it would have most definitely been Dobbs.

With the fear of God and infertility in his eyes, Dobbs reached to where his testicles were supposed to be to see if they were still attached to his body, or if they had been blown out the back of his slacks. His respirations bore a close resemblance to the gasping I did during anxiety attacks, cheeks billowing rapid-fire until, mercifully, he passed out cold right there on the fairway. *Cold.*

I looked up to find out what kind of sick animal would not yell Fore! when his ball was about to mame or kill another golfer. In the distance, I made out two teenage boys pulling their bags along the grass in a full sprint towards freedom. Even if I'd wanted to give pursuit (and I didn't) there would have been little point—they were long gone.

I leaned over Dobbs and put an ear to his mouth: still breathing. I scanned his perfectly-pressed slacks for blood and found none, front or back.

"Dobbs? You there?" I slapped him on the side of the face gently because that's how they did it to boxers on TV. "Dobbs, wake up. Wake *up.*" My slap became more of a smack until I heard him mumbling.

"Call my fence cell," he muttered with his eyes still closed.

"Huh? Call who?" I asked, leaning closer.

"My fiancée."

"Oh, your fiancée, right. What's the lucky lady's number, buddy?"

I reached for my cell phone in my back pocket.

"Front pocket of my bag, next to the box of new tees. My cell phone."

His eyes opened briefly, rolled back into his head, and closed again.

"Use your phone?" I verified.

"Hold down '1'," he said.

"Great. Great."

I reached into his golf bag and found his cell phone. I held down the number "1" and put the phone to my ear, not sure what I was going to say or how I was going to say it. *Excuse me, Miss? Yeah, the groom has just had a, um, sex change?*

"The wedding's on, no matter what," Dobbs said for me to pass on to his love.

"What's your fiancée's name?" I asked Dobbs, as the phone began to ring.

"Emily."

"Emily?"

"Emily. Emily Hutchinson."

I put the phone to my chest. The world stopped. Sweet Jesus, the odds of all this. Dobbs. Eric Dobbs. The doctor who's taking Emily from me.

"Hello? Honey? Eric?"

It was her voice. Undeniably. I wanted to drop the phone and run away like the teenagers who hit Dobbs with the golf ball, but I couldn't I was frozen. I had dropped enough of my life already and I had already run plenty far. I put the phone back to my ear.

"Tell me you're not marrying this jerk," I said.

"Who is this?"

"You know who this is," I said. "Tell me you're not *marrying* this guy."

"Tommy?"

"How 'bout this coincidence, huh?"

Dobbs opened one eye and peered up at me.

"Tommy, you've lost your mind," she said. "What are you doing to Eric? Why the hell are you *with* Eric?"

"Fate."

"What the hell is going on, Tommy?"

"No invitation to the wedding, no phone call to your boyfriend?"

"My boyfriend? You're crazy, you know that?"

The emphasis on 'crazy' struck me as unnecessary but she was right. Flashes of clarity pounded my brain. Overload. She was right. Here I was, chasing an undeserving girl that had stopped loving me long before I stopped loving her. Emily was getting *married*. This wasn't just a drunken rendezvous at an airport motel like with that dude in Florida, nor was it a spring break 'accident' like the time she may or may not have tripped and landed on a lacrosse player from Johns Hopkins in a hottub. She was signing on the dotted line for eternity with Dobbs. We were done. The realization almost made me reach for a 9-iron and lay Dobbs to rest just to spite her.

"Your fiancée, this pig, is on the ninth fairway of Alondra in a heap. You might want to get down here with a bag of frozen peas."

"What did you say? What did you do to him, Tommy!" she screamed into my ear. "Tommy! If you put one finger . . ."

Click.

"She'll be here soon, buddy," I told Dobbs.

"You know Emily?" Dobbs asked as I started to walk away.

I turned around to face him.

"No." I said. "No, I don't, dipshit."

"Tommy?" he asked, but I just kept walking.

Me and Pablo

For the next few weeks I surprisingly rarely even thought about Emily. When she did enter my mind, I grabbed her by the collar and threw her back out. Each and every time I handed her a forced exit, I was getting back small amounts of time and happiness she had stolen from me. Still, she kept coming back, knocking unbidden on the door of my consciousness, haunting my sleep. After several more weeks of this, I decided to call her. Or maybe it's not right to say I "decided," because even as I dialed her number, it felt as though someone other than me was doing it, and I was just watching.

She picked up on the third ring. "Hello?"

"By now you know I didn't do anything to your betrothed."

There was a pause, and I thought she might hang up.

"Yes," she said finally. "Eric told me what happened."

"Just plain bad luck, on his part," I said. "Or maybe something more, if you're inclined to believe in things like karma and justice."

"He doesn't owe you anything," Emily said. "And neither do I."

"Eric and Emily," I said. "I love the alliteration. You going to give all your kids 'e' names, too?"

"What do you want, Tommy?"

It was a good question. I hesitated, realizing I had no idea what I wanted, or why, really, I'd even called her.

"I want to see you," I said finally, unable to come up with anything else.

"Why?"

"Because I have to know."

She sighed. "Know what?"

"I'm not sure," I told her. "But it'll be clear once I look you in the eye."

Against all odds, she agreed to meet me at a coffee shop on Fountain in West Hollywood. Daylight, very public, lots of people around. She sat waiting at a small table by the windows when I arrived, and I stood outside looking at her before she noticed me. Her hair was longer, down past her shoulders now, and she dressed like the California kept wife she was about to become; gone were the jeans and t-shirts, replaced by fancy flowing slacks, a billowy white blouse, and short heels. I took a deep breath, went in, made sure she saw me, then took my time standing in line and ordering an iced macchiato I didn't even want one because it was complicated and required several minutes to make.

I wasn't sure if I was delaying because I was scared to go over, or because I wanted to irritate her further. Both, probably.

When I finally approached the table Emily just stared at me, somewhat balefully. I stood there a minute, looking back at her.

"Well," I said. "Mind if I sit?"

"That's what we're here for, isn't it?"

I pulled out the chair and sat opposite her.

"I hope," she said, "that this isn't going to be half an hour of you trying to convince me not to marry Eric."

"When's the blessed day?"

"Is that your business now?"

I rubbed at my eyes.

"No one's here to try and get a wedding called off. I just wanted to see you."

"You still haven't said why."

I looked at her again: same Emily, despite the wardrobe change. The same woman I'd imagined I couldn't live without. The same woman whose 4x6" photo I'd carted across the country like its existence was essential to my own. And now here we were: me chasing some pipe dream, her getting married to that simp Dobbs. What a world.

"Why did you agree to see *me*?" I asked, mostly because I had no answer for her question.

She looked away, out the window at the traffic passing in the sunlight. "It's a good question," she said. "Honestly? I think some part of me wanted confirmation I was right to leave you in the first place. And I guess I imagined seeing you would accomplish that."

"Has it?"

She looked back at me, not unkindly. "Yeah," she said. "I think it has."

"Well for what it's worth, the feeling is pretty much mutual," I said. "There's no way I could love someone who loves a guy like Dobbs."

"You don't know him, Tommy."

"That's where you're wrong," I said. "There's no better way to get to know who someone really is than playing golf with him."

"Ridiculous," she said.

"No, really. I can tell you after one round whether someone can be trusted, whether he's a good husband or dad, whether he loves his mom the way he should. Golf reveals character like nothing else."

"And what did it reveal about Eric?"

"That he's extremely unlucky."

"Ha ha."

"He's a simpleton and a narcissist, Emily. You will be very rich and very, very bored."

She didn't respond right away. Instead, she just gazed at me for several moments, then said, "And what does golf reveal about *you*, Tommy?"

I wasn't prepared for this, and I also wasn't prepared for the way I answered it with some depth.

"It reveals that I'm imperfect, but my heart's in the right place. That I'm not a cheater or a know-it-all. That I probably don't do as much as I could to be good at the things I love. That I'm a work-in-progress, like everyone else."

For the first time, Emily's face softened, and I saw a glimpse of the woman I'd known—kindhearted, gentle, forgiving.

"That you are, Tommy," she said. "That you are."

And then she got up from her seat, slung her purse over her shoulder.

"I love Eric," she said. "I've got my reasons, and they're good ones. I'm going to marry him, and we're going to be happy."

"For what it's worth," I said, "I hope that you're right. Really, I do."

And that was the last I saw of Emily, the woman I'd come to California for in the first place. She went out the door, walked past the windows, and left my life for good, a fact about which I ended up feeling much better than I ever imagined I would.

In the weeks that followed I found myself working like a man possessed. In the morning, I wrote. In the afternoon, I wrote. In the evening, I wrote. In the middle of the night, I wrote. When I wasn't writing, I was thinking about writing. In the shower, on the can, walking the streets of Hollywood, I was constructing plot, polishing characters and extending my hand and introducing myself to total strangers in search of the one connection that would give me the break I needed. Hollywood is a big cocktail party.

I joined an unofficial screenwriters club, the unofficial members of which came and went at all hours from a trendy coffee shop on Melrose. Angelina, an older flower-power type woman who never wore anything other than flowing sun skirts, was the matriarch of the group. We pulled tables together and nursed coffees, kvetched and bitched. Some of the writers probably had good reason for bitterness, but most didn't. I heard all about their near misses and the reasons their work was not being purchased, or why such and such director was blackballing them from such and such movie. I learned where to hang out, on what days, between what hours to see so and so producer in my genre, or such and such group of literary agents having cocktails. I learned how I was supposed to pitch myself and my work to hard-ass movie executives. I learned about the recent movie-making trends in Hollywood and what certain studios were looking for as far as material. I was the world's biggest sponge, soaking it all in.

Mom had remembered to put some money into my account, but the $200 she had deposited was hardly enough. With Lorazepam and Emily both gone for good, the ticking clock was getting louder and louder. In a few days I was supposed to be rich or returning home a failure. As hard as I looked, I couldn't seem to find any middle ground there.

I was finally close to actively participating in Hollywood and I was in the thick of my mission. I wasn't thinking about Emily, or the past in general. There was no time for it. I was thinking about pitches and best feet forward and the laundry list of industry protocol tidbits that the coffee shop writers had made me digest. It was exactly what I had wished for, to be in Hollywood and pursuing my dream and/or delusions, but it was scarier than Tim Wakefield in the ninth inning to actually be sitting on the corner of Sunset Boulevard with nothing but half of a cup of coffee and a crumpled twenty in my front pocket.

"Get a book of agents, write a cover letter, a one page synopsis of your script, and send a package out to anyone in the agents book who is looking for your type of script," Angelina said with a calm smile from her usual spot on the brown leather couch at the back of the coffee shop. "The process is expensive, tedious, and probably fruitless, but it's your only hope."

Angelina, as it turns out, had been around. She was collecting royalties on television scripts she sold in the 70s and 80s. The coffee shop was her brainchild for partial retirement. She had done what for us wannabes was still a pipe dream: she made a living as a writer. She was the motherly scribe who shed a realistic light on the industry for all of us aspiring folk, the herd of hungry writers who hung out at the coffee shop with our laptops and insecurities.

"A book of agents?" I asked.

"Samuel French's on Sunset. Across from Kinko's. Second level in the back under *Industry Handbooks*."

"How much?" I asked.

"Eighteen ninety-five."

Perfect. I had exactly one twenty-dollar bill in my pocket and I was in the mood to put my money where my mouth was.

"Thanks, Ang."

"You're welcome, Tommy," she said and adjusted the stick of incense on the coffee table so the aroma would pass directly under her nose.

I parked across from French's in a Kinko's-only spot and dropped a few quarters into the meter. I watched the red hand from the pedestrian light stare at me from across the street and for the first time, I really felt like I was a part of Hollywood. There was no denying the presence of it all. I wasn't in Kansas and it sure as a Larry free-throw wasn't Beantown.

I was so damn far from home, and it seemed every person in every passing car knew it. Like swarming bees, they smelled my fear. I didn't have a friend to call to go to the bookstore with me and I wouldn't have anyone to meet for a pint after I found the book. I felt liberated and nauseated all at once.

The light finally turned green and I strutted across the street, just another fool on this goose chase that thousands had done before me. I put my head down and followed my feet into French's, careful to regulate my breathing: slowly in, slowly out.

I could've spent the entire weekend in French's. They had everything under one roof that I ever wanted to read. So much knowledge, so much good advice, so much history. Screenwriters, actors, directors, and anyone else looking for their piece of the pie had their own little section in the bookstore. I got sidetracked into a copy of the *Leaving Las Vegas* script before realizing I had almost used up all my time on the parking meter. I shook my head to gather my thoughts and reminded myself to buy nothing other than what I had come to buy. I perused the section filled with industry directories until I came upon "The Agents" by casting director and career consultant Kevin Coyote. I flipped through its pages and was happy with the contact information Mr. Coyote was offering for literary agents and his own personal offer to do readings with young actors. (Note: years later I saw Kevin Coyote on a pornography industry documentary titled *Going Down in the Valley*. The guy's real job was to lure and cast incoming porn talent in L.A.).

I made sure Coyote's resource was published this year and that it clearly detailed what types of material each agent desired, as Ang said it would, and it did. I figured my script fell under the "coming of age" category, though it could have been New Age, Fiction, Non-fiction,

Young adult, Counter Culture, Modernist, Dramatic, Sci-Fi, or maybe even Autobiographical. The meter outside was running in my head so I made my way to the clerk and unloaded my twenty.

As luck would have it, and as Los Angeles parking attendants (Satan's offspring) would have it, I had a yellow ticket flapping under my windshield wiper when I returned to my car. Bastard. But the meter wasn't up yet, which meant someone in Kinko's must've realized I was illegally parked in their parking spot and called the cops. But who would do such a thing? What kind of person had such a black, shriveled heart that they would feel compelled to actually *call* the fucking meter maid on a fellow human being?

And then I saw the monster in question—a girl, sixteen or so, staring at me through the Kinko's window. I swung a hand through my shaggy, greasy hair, leaned back against my car, and lit a cigarette. I blew smoke directly towards the four-eyed brown-nosing teenage girl peering out the window. I could tell she was watching me to make sure I stayed at a safe distance. I felt kind of bad for her that she called L.A. home and didn't know how weird that was. Still, I didn't feel that bad, and besides, she'd screwed me, so I stuck my tongue out at her and wiggled it like a perverted creep, then stepped on my cigarette butt as she darted back to the safety of her register.

Katie was rehearsing her lines when I walked in. I paused at the doorway—the apartment was trashed, garbage scattered about the living room as if someone had emptied a dumpster in there.

"Find your agent book?" she asked.

"Yeah. Hey, uh, what happened here, Katie?"

"What d'ya mean?" she asked.

She watched me look around the room and still kept a smile on her face, as if the place was not strewn with refuse, or as if the fact that it was strewn with refuse was perfectly normal.

"Well, for example, why is there garbage on the floor? It wasn't here when I left two hours ago."

"Props."

"Props?" I asked.

"Props."

"Props for what?"

"My audition. I figure the grandmother is too old to keep up with the domestic side of things."

"I thought you were an aspiring director."

Katie explained that she was auditioning for the part of a grandmother in a Schwepp's ginger ale commercial. She didn't mention why she thought Schwepp's would want a twenty-nine-year-old woman to play a septuagenarian knitting a sweater in a rocking chair—or why it was strictly necessary to trash our apartment for her to get into character.

"Katie, listen, this place is plenty gross enough without dumping trash on the floor for theatrical inspiration, okay?"

I took a seat on the folding beach chair next to Katie.

"Have you talked to our new neighbors yet?" I asked her.

"The Russians? No way."

"Why not?"

"Mafia."

"Really?"

I had learned by now that a lot of what Katie said required further clarification and/or confirmation.

"There's a Russian mafia in West Hollywood. It's like Chinatown, but Russian."

"Well they're rude. I haven't gotten a single smile or head nod from one of these assholes."

"Are you smiling at them?"

"We do crazy things like that where I'm from."

"Ugh. How exhausting and pointless."

I lit a smoke and let my shoulders slip lower into the ripped beach chair.

"This is sad."

"What?"

"This apartment."

"It's nice enough."

"Says the trash throwing roommate."

"I don't throw trash. I placed it quite carefully." She was almost cute enough to let her oddities pass without judgment, but not quite.

"Do me a favor?" I said.

"Depends."

"Can we keep trash and luncheon meats and things that don't smell nice in the trash can?"

"All you have to do is ask in this world, Tommy." She jumped up to clean.

Should I really have to ask, Katie?

"You're right. You're absolutely right," I said.

close a check in the computer system. By the end of my first shift, Kimmy's assessment was that I would be okay if I learned to move just a touch quicker. But she worried that the thing I lacked—a sense of urgency—was not something that could be taught, unlike, say, the proper way to roll silverware. And she was probably right. I didn't care enough to rush around with my hair on fire, like the other servers. And I couldn't foresee a time when I would. Still, I wasn't worried about my ability to do the job well enough to avoid being fired, and that was all that mattered, ultimately.

Around midnight our last customers had finished their coffees and were walking out the door. Mikey gave me a heartfelt salute as he, too, left the restaurant after reminding Kimmy to lock up. Very trusting, I thought. Kimmy saw Mikey depart and that was her cue to leave me with instructions to take out the trash and sweep the floors before I clocked out. She was gone before I had a chance to ask any questions, like how to lock the front door when I left.

"No problemo," Pablo, a teenage dishwasher with a firecracker of a smile told me. "I help you close, amigo."

"Si, gracias," I said, relieved.

Pablo helped me find the trash bags and the broom and dustpan and we got to work.

My communication with Pablo thus far had been mostly with my hands and I wasn't really expecting us to attempt communication with real words. I hadn't spoken a word of Spanish since high school, and it was as terrible then as it is now. Luckily, Pablo had learned some English.

"You live here?" he asked.

"West Hollywood."

"Oh," he said with a big smile. "Loco, no?"

"I guess, yeah."

"Loco."

I wanted to know what he meant, exactly, but didn't know how to ask.

"How long you work here?" I asked, using as few words as possible so he might understand me.

"Dos. Two years."

"How old are you?" I said.

"Sixteen."

Like most Mexican kids in the restaurants, he was working illegally.

"Family? *Familia?*"

"In Mexico."

"No family in California?"

"No family, no," he said and his smile went from enormous to just average-sized.

"You miss them?"

"Mucho."

"You live close?"

"Yes, amigo."

"Roommates?"

"Six roommates. Two-bedroom," he said and his smile went back to enormous.

I wanted to give Pablo everything I owned in the world, but I didn't have much either, so we just cleaned and talked. I stopped probing about work and money because I knew Pablo didn't need to be reminded how hard his life had been and would continue to be. Instead, we talked about women, movies, George Bush, and just about anything that had absolutely nothing to do with paying bills and missing family.

When we were finally done cleaning, Pablo set the alarm system and we were free to leave. Moments later Pablo took his seat at the public bus stop outside the restaurant with two quarters in hand and I headed for my truck that Mommy and Daddy had sold to me for half-price to get me to and from my precious little college.

I stopped for a cheeseburger at Fatburger, then hustled home to bang out a thousand words or so before I'd slug some Smirnoff and go to bed on the egg crate.

I parked my truck a few blocks from my apartment and walked passed a group of older Russian men standing outside a steel door that led to a brick office building. The sign read "Igor Second Hand" but now I knew, courtesy Katie, that there was shady business underway behind the door, something entirely more fascinating than a thrift store.

"Evenin', ladies," I said but didn't break my stride for a response.

Behind the Curtain

Working at The Stallion certainly helped the writing process, in that it provided an endless stream of interesting stuff to riff off of. I couldn't go a single shift without meeting an individual or hearing a quote or conversation that didn't spark within me the desire to write about something. I couldn't write at home anymore, on account of Katie and her various roles, which had become more distracting and unnerving with each passing day/failed audition. So instead I spent a lot of my time at the coffee shop under Angelina's watchful eye. It was quiet enough, the coffee was strong, and my fellow members of the hopeless screenwriters club, most of whom were bullshitters, provided good entertainment. Some had some good insight into the business, though, like how to properly query an agent for representation, which I had been doing daily for three weeks. I even got a response from an agent much sooner than the coffee shop writers said I would—a fact that inspired equal amounts sincere congratulations and barely-concealed jealousy and contempt. I took both as a sign that I was getting there, however slowly.

Edward Shaw, owner and sole agent at E.J. Shaw Talent Group, decided I had a voice that could be marketable. We arranged to meet at Starbucks. How officially Tinseltown. He wanted to treat me to coffee and I was thrilled. This was my break, the moment I'd worked and waited for. Surely, once I had an agent, it was only a matter of time before everything else fell into place: I'd sell a script, make my fortune, and invite Mom and Dad to my new multi-million-dollar home in the Palisades by next Easter. Edward had survived and thrived in this world for decades, and he wanted to use what he'd learned to help me do the same.

We met on a Monday morning at a time when most people would be gearing up for lunch. This was precisely why I avoided scheduling conflicts by working nights in The Stallion. Edward looked scarily similar to Burt Reynolds in "Striptease" and talked as quickly and sugary. If I hadn't been so eager to believe he was my ticket to fame and fortune, I would probably have been a bit more skeptical of his schtick.

Edward's intro included a quick biography, which highlighted his ability to locate new talent and his close affiliation with the players in the Hollywood machine. It was all very impressive – and fast. I couldn't get a word in edgewise as he assured me that he had an eye for "the goods" and that he didn't waste his time with low-end talent. The clear implication was that I had the goods, I was high-end all the way, and I was pleased about that. Edward may have turned out to be a louse and a phony, but in one critical way he had what it took to be a successful agent: he knew what people wanted to hear.

"What do you want to be when you grow up?" Edward asked with a cocky smile, like he could provide for me whatever answer I was about to give.

"Johnny Cash circa 1968, of course," I said in an attempt to sound more cocksure than desperate.

"A lyricist over a screenwriter? Interesting choice," he mused.

"On second thought, my voice is no good. But I like his appeal to crooks."

"Well, if you want to sing at Folsom, I can't help you. What I can do, Tommy, is get you started on a writing career 'cause I think you're onto something with those twisted dream tales of yours."

A big gulp of coffee reached my lips as I inched forward in my chair.

"You do?" I asked, trying not to sound as eager and desperate as I felt.

"There's a common misconception that anyone can write, babe," Edward said. "Sure, we can all physically put a pen to paper or fingers to a keyboard, babe, but only a few *write* to us. Understand?"

"Yup," I agreed.

"Writers are not shallow slobs who waste their days dreaming of superstardom and Oscar speeches," he continued. "Dreamers dream, babe. Writers wake up, get to work, and make their own success. I might be wrong here, but I don't think you're a slob."

"I'm no slob, Edward," I said.

Or was I? I wasted untold hours dreaming of superstardom and recognition. Appeal and recognition were at least half the point for me.

Maybe I was a slob. Maybe I wasn't doing this for the right reasons. On the other hand, though, I wrote as much as a human being with a real job and normal sleep requirements could. I wasn't lazy, I knew that. So where did I land in Edward's binary of real writers and fake writers? Should I show my hand or play the role he'd assigned me? I drank my coffee, nervous that he'd see through me, see my every cell crying out for fame and fortune.

"Good. You seem a bit down, a bit tired perhaps. That's okay, babe. It either means you're lazy or hungry for better. My money's on the latter."

I nodded in silent agreement.

My attention span expired as it does. I found it odd Edward would have time in his busy schedule of hob-knobbing with the industry's future hot intellectual property to have coffee with a resume-less kid from Boston. But it's easy to believe what you want to believe, and I wanted to believe this guy was the real deal, so I swallowed my sips of coffee and the two big scoops of sugar he was spoon-feeding me. Just as I was ready to beg for a pen to sign some sort of contract, Edward slowed my roll by suggesting we meet at his office the following day to really get down to business.

All in all, I had a hunch something smelled a little funky with Shaw, but I ignored my gut feeling and strutted into his office in Studio City the next day. Under my arm were the materials he suggested I bring: 500 copies of the script synopsis (15 cents a pop on 20 lb. bond paper) and my work schedule printed out for him to see my availability.

I arrived fashionably early wearing a pressed Ralph Lauren button-down and a pleated pair of khakis, and waited in Edward's lobby for about a half hour until he skipped out of his office with a bright smile and a 5'5" blonde in dangerously high heels. A secretary, perhaps.

The phone rang and she hustled over to grab it by the second ring.

"Shaw Talent, how may I help you?" she said, thereby answering my question.

"Babe," Edward said, sitting me into a plus chair in his office. "We need to get your name on the streets."

"On the streets?"

"Yes, the streets talk around here, babe."

"And how do we get my name to the streets?" I asked.

"You write, you get published, and we tell everyone that the best writer in Hollywood, the freshest and most unique twister of tales, is none other than Tommy Rafferty. And he's ready for hire. But only at the right price."

"How do I get published?" I asked,

"Local rags, editorial type crap, your take on the scene. Write a play, get it into a theatre somewhere and invite the whole town to come see it. Write a scene for a USC student director to do for his thesis. Anything and everything, Tommy. Just get your name onto the street."

"Mr. Shaw?" the secretary asked, cautiously peeking her head into the office.

"Yes, Katrina?" Edward asked.

"Your two-thirty has arrived."

"Send him in," he said and Katrina left the room.

I felt like I was at the dentist's office.

"That's it?" I asked.

"That's it. We've got lots of work to do, Tommy, so let's get down to it, eh?"

"Sure. Sure, let's get down to it, Edward."

On my way out I passed a twenty-something guy with a towering stack of script copies on his lap as I nodded goodbye to Katrina in the waiting room. As with all the other warning signs about Edward, it was easy enough to dismiss, because I wanted—needed—to believe the bullshit he was shoveling.

I busted into the sunlight of Los Angeles, smiling. I embraced the moment. I deserved it, dammit. I had an agent. Wait until the coffee shop writers heard! Wait until my parents heard. *Sorry, mom, I can't come home for Christmas, because my agent has meetings lined up that week. My agent said I should sell a script within a year…because he's my agent…and a good agent, too.*

Edward saw something promising in me. I was clearly a special - very special - young man. I'd taken a huge chance, and now it was starting to feel like it just might pay off.

****

"Edward *Who?*" Angelina asked, when I returned triumphant to the coffee shop.

"Shaw."

"Never heard of him," she said, lighting a fresh incense stick and placing it carefully on a burner on the table in front of her.

"EJ Shaw Talent Group?" I said, still hopeful.

Angelina sat back and searched the ceiling with her eyes, thinking. After several long moments she looked back at me and said, "Nope. Still nothing."

I sat back, suddenly deflated, and sipped my coffee, which had long since gone cold.

"Don't get too discouraged, honey," Angelina said. "I've been at this a long time, but I don't know everyone, not by a long shot. There are plenty of good boutique agencies that I've never heard of. Probably."

"Probably?"

"Well, it's not likely. But it's possible."

****

Katie's Schwepps audition had come and gone a week before, so there was no reason for there to be garbage anywhere but in the trash can. But when I walked into our apartment after the stop to see Ang, there on the living room floor sat a half-eaten taco sprouting mold, flanked by a coffee filter full of grounds and a section of newspaper with a wet stain on it. I threw my bag onto the beach chair and turned my attention to the sound of crumpling paper in the kitchen. I turned on the light and nearly jumped out our only window at the sight of what was on our countertop.

Standing in front of me was a rat the size of a Volkswagen.

How big? Let's give him a sweater and a hockey stick and he could have served admirably as the mascot for the Syracuse River Rats. He could have tied his own skates, I bet.

"Katie!" I screamed. Instead of running at the sound of my voice, the rat just fixed me with a bone-chilling stare.

"*What?*" Katie asked, coming out of the bathroom.

"Shhh," I said, pointing. "Is he yours?"

Katie followed my finger with her gaze, and a second later threw a hand over her mouth.

"Holy *shit*," she said between her fingers. "He's *really* big."

"Well, if you think about it, it would take a mutant marsupial to finish the taco you left on the floor."

"What do we do?" she asked, sliding over to put me between her and our houseguest.

"Forgive me for being too obvious, but we stop leaving meat and trash all over the apartment, for starters."

"Can you kill it?" she asked.

"Too late," I said.

"Why?"

"He's already established dominance, that's why."

"Huh?"

"He's in my head," I said.

"Hit him with a broom."

"Won't work. He'll eat it then come to the source."

"How do we know it's a he?"

"Who *cares?*" I asked.

95

"I don't see any balls, is all."

"Do rats have balls?" I asked.

"My ex had 'em."

"And how did you get rid of him?"

"He left on his own, started fucking his car insurance lady."

"I've got an idea. We'll put a bigger, better prize outside. The 'ol bait and switch."

"The 'ol *what*?"

"Open the door," I told her.

"Why?"

"I'm gonna put a bag of greasy potato chips on the doorstep and tap him toward the chips with the broom."

"You can't just pick him up?" she asked.

"I don't know. He's big enough that I might need your help."

"Never mind. The broom thing will do."

I backed up, keeping my eyes on the rat, reached back for the door handle, and pushed it open. Stage one, complete. But now for the bigger challenge: getting the potato chips. Out of the cupboard. In the kitchen. Where the rat still rested, its malevolent stare fixed on me.

"As usual," I said to Katie, "I didn't think a plan through all that carefully."

"What do you mean?"

"Well if I'm going to put the potato chips outside, I have to grab the potato chips first."

"Okay."

"Which means I have to go into the kitchen…"

"Oh, don't be such a baby, Tommy."

"Why don't *you* do it?"

"Yeah, that's not happening."

We were at an impasse. The door was open, the path of escape clear. I just had to drum up the courage to get the chips. I took a couple deep breaths, then moved slowly into the kitchen, keeping my back against the wall farthest from the rat, the broom held out in front of me like the world's worst lion tamer.

"Tommy, be careful!" Katie said.

"Thanks, good thinking."

The rat followed my every movement with his gaze, which I convinced myself was a good thing: he would see the chips, and he would follow them. I flipped open the cabinet door, grabbed the bag, and immediately moved back against the wall before he could launch an attack. I basically held my breath the rest of the way out of the kitchen, got to the front door, and tossed the chips on the doorstep.

Nothing. He didn't move.

"Now what?" Katie said.

"I don't know."

We stood there, thinking, keeping an eye on the rat, who continued to perch on the counter.

"What if you did like a Hansel and Gretel thing?" Katie asked.

"Meaning?"

"You know. Bread crumbs."

I was skeptical, but had no better ideas myself. So I picked the bag up again, went back into the kitchen, sprinkled a line of chips from the counter to the front door, then dumped the rest out on the doorstep.

At first, King Rat still refused to budge, and I wondered, briefly, if we would have to move out and cede the place to him. But then the siren song of Lay's Wavy Hickory BBQ proved too much, and he executed a startlingly acrobatic dismount from the countertop, clinging to drawer handles on the way down, and started munching on the first chip I'd placed on the floor.

"This is going to be a while," I said to Katie. "Drink?"

"Double vodka," she said, not looking away from our houseguest.

For an hour we sat side by side on the edge of my bed, nursing extra stiff vodka-Gatorades and watching as the rat slowly but steadily made his way through the living room and finally, mercifully, out into the parking lot. I slammed the door shut when he was gone, thereby bringing to a close the most harrowing experience Katie and I would have as roommates.

But it didn't take long, after we successfully convinced the rat to go outside, for Katie to forget all about the ordeal. That very night, in fact, she left a plate of half-eaten rice pilaf on the counter. Irritated and exhausted, I scooped the rice into the trash after she was asleep on her cot, thinking this arrangement couldn't go on much longer.

Katie and West Hollywood were testing my patience and my resolve. It had been months since I'd first driven into town, and all I had

to show for it was waiter's tips and a roommate who refused to put trash
in   the   trash.

Ends and Means

As I headed to my locker in the back of the restaurant after a jog, Mikey the Manager passed me at a trot and muttered, "Wash up, get dressed, and make sure you tuck your shirt in, Tommy. Be ready in five."

"I can't do all that in five."

"Then take a whore's bath in the sink. I need you on the floor in five minutes. And I'm timing you."

"What's the rush?"

"Just do it," he said and bolted into his office behind the locker area.

"Fine, relax," I said to no one in particular, wondering what had Mikey so tense.

I headed to the bathroom to splash a couple handfuls of cold water onto my face, not in any more of a rush than I normally would be. Pablo approached, looking tense himself, but given his poor English and my worse Spanish, he couldn't tell me what was going on. He simply bugged his eyes out, smiled hugely, and patted my shoulder.

Now I started to worry a little bit. Pablo was normally more laid-back; if he was worked up about something, there had to be a good reason.

And here came Mikey the Manager again, with me still in my boxers.

"Tommy," he said, "I told you five minutes."

"And it's been three."

"It's been *seven*," he said. "Get your clothes on and get out there, or I'm sure I can find someone else who'll be happy to wait on Kevin Costner."

He was gone again before I could ask him to confirm what he'd just said.

Two minutes later Mikey saw me approaching the dining area from the bathroom and skirted over to meet me halfway from his hosting station located by the front door.

"You're the best I have tonight, Tommy, so I have to go with you," Mikey said.

"Excuse me, but what, the hell, is going on here?"

He looked at me, incredulous.

"Did you not hear me the first time?" he asked, grabbing my shoulders and steering me toward the dining room. "Look, just remember that Mr. Costner likes his water without ice."

When I was seven, I found a duffle bag with a thousand dollars in the woods and then got caught trying to put it into the bank an hour later. (The bank teller, who happened to be on the PTA with Mom, thought I was "as cute as a button, like a miniature stock broker," but that didn't stop her from notifying my parents of my unexplained wealth.) No one ever questioned my story or called me a thief, but they still didn't let me keep the money. My Dad took the cash to the police station to return to its rightful owner, and I never even heard if the rightful owner got it back. So much for being rewarded for honesty. On what universal plane does one find himself on a golf course in California, get paired at random with the fiancé of the girlfriend he wanted back? These things happen to me, and to me only, I'm sure of it. I can't explain it. They just do.

Point is, middle ground rarely exists for me when it comes to the fickleness of fortune, and the cash-in-the-woods fiasco was the start of it all. My luck is always either really good, or really, really bad. There's never any in-between. And tonight, obviously, it was really good—Kevin Costner, my Hollywood doppelganger according to Hurst in Cleveland, was for some reason eating dinner at the Stallion, and I'd been assigned to wait on him.

I skipped like a schoolgirl back to the bathroom to stare at my image in the mirror above the sink and to recite the various icebreaking sentences and anything remotely interesting in my creative arsenal that might excite Costner. I remembered one thing my uncle Bill had told me when I was a little kid. He said, "Tommy, a man prefers to answer a question that allows for his opinion."

So: what questions could I ask that demonstrated I was not another airhead wannabee like the ones Costner had undoubtedly already encountered today, yesterday, the day before yesterday, and every day for the last twenty-odd years? What question would get his attention and make him realize I was much more than just a waiter with a screenplay, like every other waiter in this town? Should we talk movies? Judging by his movie credits, I knew Costner liked sports. I knew he must have an affinity for baseball, in particular. "Bull Durham" was his baseball masterpiece and it was the flick that introduced me to Susan Sarandon, which gives it extra glory. Should we talk Cal State Fullerton baseball, or maybe Coach Oggie's move to Texas? Of course, I wanted to mention Hurst, but I always felt that name-dropping was too cliché, too depth-challenged to ignite viable conversation outside of the name being dropped.

I splashed more cold water on my face as my mind raced for the perfect line of questioning. If I had just been able to catch a little shuteye after the run on the Strand, my mind would be more focused and creative. But that was neither here nor there, at this point. I had to get back out on the floor, and whatever I ended up saying—good or bad, smart or stupid, interesting or insipid—I'd have to come up with on the fly.

I made my way to the dining room just in time to see Kevin Fucking Costner. The hourglass turned and the clock starting running. I was aware, vaguely, that my whole body had suddenly become sheened in sweat.

Costner was with another man in his early fifties or so, dressed like an accomplished businessman of some type in a navy silk suit and dazzling tie of countless colors. Kevin was a bit more relaxed in jeans, loafers, a brown t-shirt and a black sport coat. The restaurant gave a collective gasp as Costner's golf-tanned face was spotted and scrutinized for confirmation. I must say, the man looked marvelous. Not only was he casual to the point of James Dean coolness, he obviously didn't give a hoot that he was famous or being studied by all of us. He seemed to know it came with the territory. He probably didn't care for the attention, but he accepted it, and it showed as he avoided eye contact with an "aw shucks" appeal in his sure-footed strut to his reserved table. He could have been acting, of course, but I doubted it. Here was a man comfortable in his skin and his circumstances. He wore fame well. And I had to get to him, one way or another.

Game-time had suddenly arrived.

I had never, ever in my life felt so naked and small.

My tray of waters and bread rattled with each step as I walked to the table on legs weak with nerves. I could feel the eyes of everyone, my jealous coworkers in particular, and I was not handling the attention nearly as well as Costner had. Hurst had been wrong; I was no Costner in the making. Maybe this is why I didn't want to be an actor and preferred to write my way to celebrity.

"Welcome to the Stallion," I said and placed the waters and bread safely in front of Kevin and Rich Friend.

"Hey, pal, thank you," Costner said with a broad smile.

Holy shit, he sounds just like Kevin Costner.

His relaxed manner should have put me at ease but I remained a boner in sweatpants, swaying in clear sight and with no clear purpose. For a painfully long moment I struggled to say something, anything, but I just couldn't do it. Suddenly, I knew less English than Pablo and my college degree wasn't worth a red cent. Rich Friend felt my stare and afforded me a courteous, yet confused, smile. Costner, on the other hand, must have been unfazed by my awkward presence because he just continued to read the menu without any change in demeanor. Finally, I turned my body in the other direction and began to walk back to the kitchen, realizing as I went that I'd forgotten to tell them about the specials. *Shit. Shit, shit, shit.*

Mikey peered at me from the front of the restaurant, seemingly knowing—or assuming—I had fucked up my one and only table. I took a deep breath, turned around, and made my way back to Kevin and Rich Friend.

"Gentlemen, let me add, please, that we have two specials today," I said, marveling even as I spoke that I was suddenly able to form words. "First, we have salmon ravioli, covered in a nice, pink sauce, a combination of both marinara and alfredo."

I couldn't believe I had Kevin Costner's attention. He was looking at me. In fact, his eyes were locked onto mine. He may have even been listening to the words coming out of my mouth.

"Secondly, we have Ciapino, which is a seafood stew, with clams, calamari, salmon, halibut and shrimp in a spicy red stew and a side of garlic toast."

"Sounds good. Give us a minute here to look things over?" Kevin said.

I walked away, waited exactly sixty seconds like my friend Kevin had asked, then returned to the table to take their order.

Rich Friend wanted the Pasta Primavera. To my delight, Costner went with the Ciapino, a clear indication that he had, in fact, been listening to me. But any opportunity to talk to him about something other than seafood stew vanished—before I'd even finished scribbling their orders onto my notepad, they resumed their conversation, ignoring me entirely.

A writer can never know when the time will come, where it will come, or how long you'll have to make your pitch. You won't know the mood of the person listening or what the person may want to hear, if anything at all. The challenge is to sell your writing and yourself in a very brief time frame to someone who is very busy and inclined to not give a shit. After years of hearing stupid pitches, these are people who come armed with every excuse why they shouldn't like what you have to say before you even open your mouth. So what did knowing this mean to me? Not much. Because the only thing worse than a pitch that goes badly is a pitch that doesn't happen at all.

I stood by the cook's station and rubbed my chin, hoping for inspiration, and I noticed Gino, the disgruntled middle-aged line cook, glaring at me with his lazy eye. When Gino's fucked-up eye fell on you, that meant your order was coming up soon, which meant, in turn, that I had very little time to figure out what to say to Costner before I returned to the table.

I still hadn't come up with anything by the time Gino tossed my plates into the window. I decided it was better to just drop off the food and think some more while Costner and Rich Friend dug in, so I took a deep breath, balanced the tray of food on my hand, and did my job. I dropped the food with the bare minimum of interaction—fresh grated parmesan, all set on drinks, need anything else?—and retreated out back to see Pablo and collect my thoughts.

"Esta bien, asshola?" Pablo asked, clearly aware that everything was not bien.

My mind raced down two paths. On the one path, I was contemplating what Mr. Costner wanted to hear. On the other, I was contemplating what I needed to say. How could I make the two meet and marry? I stood there, gears turning, for five full minutes until a busboy came around the corner and said the two men needed more water. The clock was winding down, and I still had nothing.

I arrived at the table sweating like a pig. I cleared my throat too loudly. I wiped my brow and took an enormously deep breath. I did pretty much everything, in fact, except for actually pouring them more water. Instead, I placed the water pitcher on the table and stood there looking down at Costner. It was time, for better or for worse. Mr. Kevin Costner looked up at me after wiping his lips with a napkin and I got the feeling he knew a question totally out of context was making its way out of my gut. Oddly enough, he didn't fight it or turn away. Instead, he rested his fork on his plate, leaned back in his chair, and folded his hands across his belly.

"Mr. Costner?" I asked.

Costner nodded, allowing me to continue.

I had no idea what I was going to say until the words were already out of my mouth. "Is it worth it?" I asked.

Costner shared a smirk with his cohort and turned to me with an expression that made clear he was impressed, or at least pleasantly surprised by the unique nature of the question. I smiled, sure he was about to tell me I had balls or originality. Rich Friend chuckled and tucked back into his Primavera.

"Put some thought into what's worthwhile for *you*," Costner instructed.

"A thought that haunts me," I said, surprised that I said it aloud.

"It haunts everyone, especially at your age, kid."

It was hard to imagine that Kevin Costner could relate to anyone's uneasiness with their future prospects.

"Thank you for your advice," I said. I lifted the pitcher and filled their glasses, finally, then walked away. I didn't speak again to Costner for the rest of his meal until the very end, after he had paid his bill, tipped generously, and stood to leave.

"Hurst in Cleveland says hello," I blurted out as my last hope of establishing a bond.

Costner looked at me like I had sprouted a second head.

"You're kidding me," he said, looking at Rich Friend utterly flabbergasted.

"No, I'm not, actually. I met him in Cleveland on my drive out here."

"Forget every word he told you."

"Really?"

"The man is pure fiction. He can talk the skin off a potato with his bullshit."

"I see."

I looked down in thought as Kevin walked away, but then he turned back, catching me off-guard.

"Good luck," he said, "find the end, and then the means, kid."

Words   that   would   never   leave   me.

Decisions

My eyes could hardly believe the reality they thought they were seeing. Katie was dressed in a pilgrim's suit and had what I hoped was chocolate smeared across her front teeth, an amateurish and utterly disgusting attempt to mimic the effects of poor dental hygiene.

She walked towards me with a slutty smirk and a hickory walking cane that was apparently meant to help her character augment a recent injury of sorts.

"Mr. Rafferty? Mr. Thomas Rafferty?" the pilgrim asked as she got closer and closer to me with the hand-carved cane.

A half-smile came across my mouth but it was much more fear than amusement. In recent weeks I'd begun to genuinely question whether Katie was mentally well, and these sorts of antics didn't seem to support the notion.

"Katie? Are you okay, sweetheart?" I asked.

"Ooh, *sweetheart*, I like that," she said.

"Is this some kind of acting preparation or rehearsal or something?"

As flattering as it should be to be seduced, roleplaying wasn't really my thing, and I found myself not in the mood for sex for perhaps the first time since I was capable of having sex. It was all a click too weird. It's one thing to sleep with someone who has a few screws loose, another thing entirely to then live with her.

Removing her white bonnet made of loose-leaf paper and staples, Katie looked me up and down slowly, as if she had never seen a guy in boxer shorts.

"They didn't make them like this in Olde England," she said.

"Did you get your hands on some bad acid?" I asked.

"My husband is working the cornfields, the children are busy at study."

"What children?" I asked, looking to see if the front door was locked. It wasn't and I briefly thought about making a run for it.

Katie slid the hooked end of her hickory cane up my leg, hooking into my tailbone, and I was suddenly certain that she wasn't acting at all. She was not playing a character; she was the character.

"Katie, look, I just had a weird dream but this is weirder, by a long shot, a really, really long shot."

"Katie?" she asked.

I had been meaning to check Katie's medicine cabinet because I'd begun to suspect that her antics, more often than not, were less about acting and more about bad wiring in her head. I reached down between my legs and pulled the hook away from my groin.

"Stop, Katie."

"Augustine," she corrected me.

111

"Okay, Augustine, I am going to go into the bathroom and you are going to stay right here. When I get back, your farming husband will be home and the kids will be enjoying afternoon snacks. Warm bread, ear of corn turkey leg, whatever you want to serve."

I headed to the bathroom at a slow place, keeping my eyes on her to make sure she wasn't following me. Once I had the bathroom door locked, I began to search for signs that Katie was officially off her rocker.

The shelves behind the vanity mirror above the sink housed nothing but normal, everyday over-the-counter medicines and a couple near-empty tubes of toothpaste without caps. Ordinary stuff. Then I noticed, for somehow the first time, a small compartment in the wall behind the bathroom door, sort of like where one might hide a safe. I had been living in the motel for long enough that it seemed impossible I hadn't clued into its existence. But I hadn't.

I turned the copper knob to the closet and found a plastic storage bin not much bigger than a shoebox. Under a smorgasbord of female products and sewing supplies, I found what I was looking for, evidence that left no doubt.

The book in the plastic bin was titled, *The Multiple Mind: An Explanation for DID (Dissociative Identity Disorder)* and the prescription pill cases under the book were full of psychiatric medications. Zoloft. Paxil. Centrax. Tranxene. Restoril. I nearly popped one of the pills from the case marked 'anxiety' into my mouth, then thought better of it. I closed the closet quietly, opened the bathroom door, and took a slow walk back into the living room now that the diagnosis was confirmed, dreading the conversation to come.

But when I entered the living room, it was empty. Katie was gone, the front door wide open. Initial relief quickly gave way to anxiety, as I imagined poor Katie walking up Sunset Boulevard dressed like Christopher Columbus' wife. She wasn't in her right mind, and West Hollywood was not a great place to have a nervous breakdown (one could argue, of course, that it's a great place to have a nervous breakdown, since you'd find so many others in the same predicament, but you get what I'm saying). I was worried about her safety but I knew this was above my pay grade, and I couldn't handle whatever was happening with her on my own.

So I did something I'd never done before in my life: called the cops.

"9-1-1, please state your emergency."

I hesitated. Did this actually fit the definition of an "emergency"?

"Uh, I think my roommate is having a nervous breakdown."

"Is your roommate male or female?"

"Female."

"And how is she behaving that makes you think she's mentally unstable?"

"Well, she's gone now, so I don't know how she's behaving at the moment," I said. "But she doesn't seem to know who she is. I think she may have a split personality, or something."

"Do you know where she went?"

"No idea," I said. "She just walked out the front door a couple of minutes ago. We live in West Hollywood."

"Was she threatening you?" the dispatcher asked. "Is she a danger to herself or others?"

"Nothing like that," I said. "She thinks she's a pilgrim."

"A pilgrim." It wasn't a question.

"I told you, she doesn't seem well in the head."

"Sir, unless your roommate is making threats, or is a danger to herself, there's not much we can do."

"Nothing at all? I just don't like the idea of her wandering around out there."

"It's not illegal to be crazy, sir."

She had me there; my dad was a cop, and he'd dealt with enough lunatics who he couldn't arrest for being lunatics. I sat on the beach chair in our living room for a prolonged moment, horrified that this poor girl had books to study her own sickness in hopes of improvement. Maybe her parents, a doctor – someone - had given her a book in a last-ditch effort to help her. And she was now in one of the more unforgiving, dangerous places on earth to embark on such an endeavor. Drugs, poverty and opportunistic predators were at every turn. But I simply didn't have the skillset to fix Katie. And it wasn't going to happen today, anyway; it was obviously going to be a long process to get her well. Besides, I had bigger fish to fry at the moment—a meeting with Cherrie Leblanc that afternoon.

****

As far as Edward Shaw had told me, Cherrie Leblanc was the cat's meow for one of the biggest cats in Hollywood, a little movie making enterprise known as Miramax. Edward couldn't say which movies she had actually produced, but he assured me the list was long and distinguished and that I better be ready to shine. These opportunities rarely presented themselves, especially to a relatively new kid in town. I had spent some time working on a pitch, so I felt like I had a good grasp on the plot and purpose of my script, but I was not completely ready for a meeting of this caliber.

I left the hotel wearing an elbow-patched wool sport jacket that I bought for six bucks at a thrift store off Highland. I stopped for coffee at Starbuck's around ten-thirty to load up on caffeine for the meeting that was to start in one hour in an office outside the studio lot. The drive was only twenty minutes, according to MapQuest, but I knew better than to trust that estimate. Taking traffic and my slow driving into account, I decided it was in my best interest to head to Cherrie's office a bit earlier than strictly necessary.

On the way I dropped the blistering hot coffee all over my white button-down shirt and enjoyed a solid thirty seconds of both pain and frantic calculations, ultimately trying to figure out if I had enough time to double back and get a clean shirt. I decided that I didn't have time to circle back home, so I just buttoned up my sport coat and hoped for good lightning.

Cher, as she insisted I call her, had one of the largest personalities I had ever met and she had yet to tell me anything but her name. Her hair was phenomenal. My older sister Stacy rocked the "jersey claw" bangs for much of middle and high school, perfecting it into an art form with enough hairspray to clear out our house, but it was never anything close to the tidal wave looming atop Cher's forehead. An AquaNet masterpiece. A functional shovel if you turned her upside down. The overall impression Cher gave was of a Dolly Parton caricature – huge boobs, wild hair, and a sparkling cocktail dress with shiny royal blue sequins. Everything about her was on a large scale, except her office. It was the size of a shoebox.

"Coffee?" she asked.

"No, thanks, had some already."

I figured that the movie posters on a movie exec's wall might indicate what you need to know about the state of their career. If the posters are of movies that were released in the early eighties and the stars of those movies had long since been shuffled out of the business, that's a bad sign. Cherrie had four posters: "Howard the Duck," "No Holds Barred," "G.I. Joe: the Movie," and "Invaders from Mars." The only actor I recognized on any of the posters was Hulk Hogan. Needless to say, alarm bells.

"So, how's Miramax treating you?" I asked. "I heard from Edward that they are *the* studio to work for in town. You didn't want their Sunset office? It's right next door to a famous hot dog stand." I had never even eaten at Carney's but I had seen its billboard the day before advertised as "famous."

"Miramax?" she said and scratched her forehead.

"Yes, Edward says you've done quite well at Miramax."

"Bastards fired me in '89 after the Duck sequel proposal," Cherrie said.

I tried to cover my surprise and dismay.

"Their loss, huh?" I asked, though pretty sure it was her loss.

"I can't seem to get anything really fabulous in the works since Duck."

"Since "Howard the Duck", you mean?"

"Should have done the sequels. Everybody loves the sequel and the trilogy. It's product recognition. Product alignment. Why switch to fries when you love the nuggets, right?"

I wasn't in the mood to play psychologist. I wanted to sell my script to Miramax and here I was realizing that Cherrie hadn't worked for Miramax since I was graduating seventh grade. But I would settle for whomever it was that Cherrie was now working. Dad was calling that evening for an update.

"So, Tommy, what's your script about?" she finally asked.

The awkwardness was killing me. But now that it was evident Cherrie had no clout, I wasn't nervous in the least about pitching.

"You ever have a dream that comes true?" I asked her.

"A dream that comes true?"

"Yeah, you know, you maybe have dreamed of some tall, dark, strapping young man in a bar and then you see him at a bar a couple nights later."

"I can't say that I go to bars."

"Okay, well, have you ever had dreams that clearly are trying to tell you something, like the way you should live your life, as opposed to the way you're living it now?"

"I guess. Well, no, I don't think so, actually."

"No offense, Cherrie, but most people do have these types of dreams where their subconscious is telling a story, guiding them to live a particular way in their waking lives. Synchronicity, it's called."

"Tommy, I think there's been some confusion. I do real-life, heartfelt movies."

"What about Duck?"

"Duck saves kids from alien invaders. That's the tagline. Heartfelt."

"But it's a Duck."

"Is it?" she asked.

"It isn't?"

"Or is it deeper than that?"

"Are we really doing this?"

"I'm an independent producer," she stated.

"And your other job?"

"What other job?"

"The one that feeds you."

Her eyes widened and she fidgeted with a pen on her desk.

"Oh, well I supervise scripts on the side."

I picked up my leather case and stood to leave, already thinking about the exact angry words I was going to say to Edward.

"So you charge writers to critique their scripts after you tell them their work won't sell?" I asked.

"Tommy, how dare you come in here and-

"Call your bluff? What's next, a price sheet for feedback on my script? How much per page, per word?"

"I think you should go."

"Well, we agree on something. Have a good one, Cherrie."

"Tell Edward to forget his check this month."

"Excuse me?"

"Yeah, you go tell Edward that his writers are too narrow-minded for Hollywood. You'll never work with George Lucas like I did. I'm tired of getting you writers from Edward who don't want help with their scripts. You all think you know everything there is to know about the biz. And you'll keep believing that, even after you fail like the rest."

"You worked with George Lucas?"

"Duck."

"No shit," I said, momentarily impressed.

"No shit," she said.

When I got in the truck, I immediately called Edward to find out if he really intended to sell my scripts, or if he was just using me in an editing for hire scheme with imposters like Cherrie.

"Cherrie said that?" Edward asked.

"She did, Edward, and I think I believe her."

"Look, she may not be at Miramax as we speak, at this moment, but she's been there before and she'll be there again."

"Edward, I think there's been a mistake."

"Oh?"

"I'm smarter than this and it's going to cause you some problems."

"Tommy, you've already got another meeting."

Curveball.

"With who?"

"Look, you just get some sleep and a nice meal. Forget about Cherrie. It's my fault. She's a fraud and I should have known it. I told you it wasn't going to be easy, did I not? You can trust me. She helps young writers with their scripts, sure, but I thought her connections were stronger than they are. My fault entirely, Tommy."

"Who's the meeting with?"

"It's a biggie, Tommy. Real big biggie. It's in the works, baby, for sure. For sure. Absolutely. We'll talk more later . . . gotta run . . . .bye."

Fuck chicken soup. This writer's soul needed a shot of Jack.

The Snake Pit on Melrose was the darkest hiding spot of a bar I could find. Either a careless or blind person cleaned the beer glasses and the bartender had something dark and dirty caked under her fingernails. But the beer tasted as it should and was cold and wet enough to satisfy my thirst. Besides, I had no interest in being at the motel. I was worried about Katie, and hoped in the abstract that she would come home unharmed, but I also didn't necessarily want to be there when she did, and didn't want to push my luck by spending more time there than was absolutely necessary.

"Are you going back or not?" the bartender asked, her pointy elbows dug into the bartop in front of me. Her dyed black hair and angry piercings about her face and ears were disconcerting, but I liked that she showed genuine interest in my frown.

"Not sure," I said.

"What's different about it?"

"Boston?" I asked.

"Yeah. I mean, what can you have at home that you can't have here?" she asked.

"A lot of things."

"Give me one."

I liked bartenders who made an effort at conversation, so I gave the question some real thought.

"I know where everything is and I don't need a Thomas Guide in my lap when I go out for groceries," I said.

"That's too easy. What else?"

"Too easy?"

"Way too easy. This is L.A. Whether you grew up here or not, nobody knows where anything is."

"Chowder on the Cape in July."

"You miss *chowder*? I ask you what you miss about living somewhere, and the best you can come up with is soup?"

She smiled, revealing a surprisingly nice, straight set of teeth. I paused for a moment, considered whether she was right, then decided she wasn't.

"Yes. I miss chowder, all right? And I miss flannel shirts and union suits and saving my parking spot with a beach chair."

"A beach chair?"

Now I was really warming up to my subject. Talking about home felt reassuring, seemed to indicate that my disconnect from the world was not *that* big, and that I kind of belonged somewhere.

"When you wake up early to shovel your car out of the snow so you can get to work on time, you reserve the right to the spot with objects until the next time it snows."

"And you save it with a beach chair?" she asked, shaking her head as if this were the strangest, most nonsensical thing she'd ever heard.

"Or a yellow cone or a milk crate. My neighbor Joanie uses a sandwich board stand that says 'keep moving' in chalk."

"You don't live there anymore. She's not still your neighbor."

"No," I said. "But she's still there. Still using her sandwich board, no doubt."

"Unless, of course, you move back into the same neighborhood you lived in before, but what good would that do for you?"

"I'd feel a part of something, that's all."

The bartender laughed like I was the dumbest man ever to come to Hollywood. And that says a lot, I'm sure.

"Distance is fooling you into believing something that isn't true."

"What do you mean?"

"What I mean is that you left home for a reason, probably because you *didn't* feel a part of anything, right? You come to L.A., you start to miss home like everyone does at first, and now you've got yourself half-convinced that Boston has somehow become Shangri-La in your absence. What you need to do is tell everyone back home to step

122

the fuck back and let you live out here. You don't want to be a deathbed sap."

"A deathbed sap, that's an interesting one," I said.

"Yeah, someone who lies on their deathbed and regrets all the things, or maybe that one big thing, that they never did."

This was getting a little too heavy, but I was still thirsty.

"Another beer, please" I said, handing her my empty pint.

"You got it."

The Goth bartender headed for the row of beer taps at the other end of the bar, as I envisioned myself old and shriveled on a bed in a tiny hospital room, staring up at a white popcorn ceiling, looking back over the life I had lived.

When I got back to the apartment it was obvious that Katie had been there, because she'd left what seemed like a dozen loads of laundry spread about the place, mostly on the floor. Even my bed was piled up with her clothes. Perhaps she got interrupted in the middle of folding and had to bolt, maybe there was an emergency even, but whether she had a good reason or not, I was still irritated by the mess. I was glad she had returned home from her New World pilgrim adventure in one piece, but I'd just about reached the end of my rope with her slovenliness.

It was only eight o'clock, but I was zonked. I had spent the entire afternoon in the Snake Pit, then wandered drunk among the human wreckage in the streets, huffing my cigarettes and thinking about the meaning of me. I called on all my will to stay positive. I figured if I fell asleep now, I could wake up early and try again to make lemonade out of this pile of shit. I heard the phone buzz as I dozed off, saw it was my father on the screen of my flip phone, and let it keep ringing. I didn't know how to tell Dad that I was entrusting my immediate future to the 5-cent wisdom of a bartender I had just met.

Beach Times

Edward didn't call like he had promised, so I perused Backstage West, a local rag for the entertainment industry, and set up three meetings on my own. All three meetings, according to the classified ads, would be with independent directors in need of a good script to shoot. Maybe this was the way I'd get my break—finding the right people to collaborate with on my own. It certainly couldn't produce less than Edward had.

After a solid week of editing the script and catching up on my sleep, I got stood up at a restaurant in the Beverly Center by one of the directors, and a last-minute cancellation from another. The latter had a dramatic change of heart and had decided to pursue a career in door-to-door cosmetic sales, foregoing the "in" at Lionsgate Films that she was so excited about when we'd first talked on the phone. At least she'd called and saved me a trip down to Long Beach.

I almost cancelled on the third director, Rod Zoob, out of spite for the first two no-show nitwits, but decided there was no point in cutting off my nose to spite my face.

On Tuesday morning I found myself at lunch with Rod in Palm Springs. He had another meeting in Palm Springs that morning so I offered to make the drive out 10W and meet him at his convenience. It was a nice drive, actually, about 2 hours through some interesting towns. One was called Cucamonga and I put on Pride of Cucamonga for effect from a Grateful Dead CD that was slotted into my sun visor CD holder.

"So tell me about your script," Rod said, finally, twenty minutes after we'd shaken hands at the posh Fletcher's Bar and Grill.

"I think you'd like it," I said, spreading a napkin on my lap at our outside table under the white gazebo. "You ever have a dream that comes true, like-

"Man, did you see "Thirteen" yet? I swear, those fuckers must have followed my life," Rod said, taking a long drag from a Marlboro. He'd been interrupting me, over and over, ever since we'd arrived, and it was starting to get under my skin.

"No, haven't seen it, Rod," I said flatly.

"USC director, I think. You know, when I was at USC we had like fifty graduates in my class alone whose names I see roll in the credits now. All of them – directors, producer, actors – amazing what that school churns out for talent."

Pausing to study Rod for a moment, I was confident that an uninterested, infinitely ungrateful brat was before me, wasting my time and precious gas money. He did it all with designer clothes, slicky dark hair, and a smile straight out of a Brooks Brothers catalogue. Not my type.

"USC, huh?" I asked, but it was more of a statement than a question. Rod was thrilled to answer, of course. I have no idea what I asked.

"Oh yeah, man. Only way to go. My dad wouldn't have it any other way."

"That's great. Good for you."

"I mean, where else can you get your diploma and win at Sundance in the same year?" he asked.

"Cool. Your dad in film?"

"Oh yeah, man. All over it. Like top talent agent for twenty years. Lives in Palm Springs now with his wifey – not my mom. Drops like *two-gee* at Santa Anita every day on the ponies."

As much as I wanted to hear about his father's gambling habits, I was determined to find out if this kid was anything more than a bored trust-fund baby.

"You working on anything now, directing?" I asked.

"Now? Naw, man," he said. "When I got back from Cannes last year, I needed a break. Just starting to dabble again, kid."

"That's great. Cannes, huh? You directed a film that made the cut?"

"Yeah, well, no, not exactly, kid. My roommate at USC worked as a grip on a short and I tagged along. Dad's still looking for my name in those credits! *Where's my money for that trip to Cannes?*"

Rod had gone from a promising, eccentric director-type at first glance to a delusional twenty-six-year-old child living in his father's posh basement.

"Rod, do you want to hear about this script I wrote, maybe see if it's something we might want to explore together?" Just as I said that, a good-looking mother crossed the street with her children. I lost Rod again.

"Rod, if you want to do this another time, that's not a problem with me. Really, let's do this another time."

"Sure, man, sure, another time is fine, I understand," he said, totally unaware of what I had just said, still undressing the woman with his eyes. I wanted to slap him upside the head. "Hey, man," he continued, "you think she'd want to get with me while her kids are in daycare? I had this teacher at USC, she was like forty and I used to-

"I gotta run, Rod, thanks."

Rod finally looked in my direction as I stood to leave. Perhaps he was surprised to be interrupted, maybe even offended. Like I cared.

"Hey, man. Good chattin'," he said. "I'll give you a call if I'm interested in your dream idea, okay? Let me see what the old man says, kid."

Kid? Make that *three* no-show nitwits from Backstage West.

****

Given everything that was going on with Katie, not to mention just the general state of things at the roach motel and the succession of fruitless script meetings, leaving West Hollywood to join Rich Mazzano in Hermosa Beach sounded pretty good to me.

Dad had listened intently to my plans to shack up with Rich and even assured me that I was a man in control of his own destiny. I could hardly believe my ears. Something felt different in our relationship, like I was growing up and he could see it. Dad had never seemed to believe I was in control of anything, let alone something as massive and slippery as my destiny, and now, out of the clear blue, he not only believed it, but actually brought himself to say it. No mention at all of the two-month timeframe I had long since blown past.

College Senior Falls Three Stories, Fighting For Life. That was the headline from the Life section of *USA Today* the morning after Rich nearly checked out when he fell from our three-story apartment window into the snow below, catching his head on the side of a parked car on his way down. We learned from his accident, among other things, that taking Sudafed and chasing it with a 12-pack of Mickey's to relieve a pulled hamstring is a bad idea, as it distorts your reality and can make you delusional. There were times watching Rich lying in a coma for three weeks that I thought he was a goner, and it was the most sobering episode I'd ever been through in my life. I was lucky to have never lost a close friend in my youth, so watching Rich struggle to stay alive was difficult.

But we should have known that, Rich being Rich, he had other plans that didn't include expiring quietly in a hospital bed. He pulled through, did his rehabilitation and physical therapy vigorously, and by the time we graduated college a few months later, he had more or less gotten back to normal. In the process, he'd grown tired of simply being "the soccer player kid who fell out the window," so he packed his stuff and let college fade in his rear-view mirror, heading for the west coast, where no one knew him or what he'd been through. Given Rich's sudden departure from my life after the fall and graduation, I never expected him to call me, and I really didn't expect he would be pissed that I was in California and hadn't called him. But he was, or at least pretended he was. I recognized his bullshit quickly as amateur hour at The Reverse Psychology Lounge, so I played along, feigning regret and shame, before accepting his invitation to pay him rent and rekindle our roommate status. A week or so later, I arrived at Rich's with my modest amount of belongings.

I parked my car in the driveway of his recently purchased two-story, three-on-a-lot townhouse. I was flat-out impressed. I knew places like this in this area of Southern California weren't cheap—he needed in the ballpark of fifty grand minimum for a down payment.

"Did you child-proof those windows up there?" I said, spreading my arms to offer a hug to my old buddy. I was surprised, and pleasantly so, at how good it felt to see him again.

"Child-proof and idiot-proof, perfect for me," he said, indicating he had developed some humility over the past few years.

I thought of Rich sporadically at best since college, but just seeing his face reminded me why I liked him. He was selfish, cocky, and had tried to kiss Emily once when I was in the bathroom at the bar, but that's just because his rich parents never told him no. About anything. He drove a Land Rover in college and had at least 10 pairs of new sneakers at all times, all bankrolled by his pops. He was one of those people who on paper should make you want to murder them. But there was something refreshing about Richie's candid nature and I never took most of his bullshit seriously, anyway.

"Romland has me on a contract from the Texas plant. Two more years minimum. They don't have a clue how I'm spending my rent stipend," he explained as we toured his place.

"So, Romland and I will pay your mortgage and you tell girls you own a condo on the beach?"

"Precisely," he said. Richie never really minced words, unless there was a clear benefit to lying, in which case he minced.

"You've got a great room upstairs, Raff. You'll love it. Five hundred a month, right?"

"Four hundred."

"Right. Four hundred. My mistake."

Having attended private school and a cushy university, I have befriended many children of great luck. I say 'luck' because these kids, driving big, beautiful SUVs and sporty BMWs, were simply lucky they were born into money and privilege. No skill required to do so. Most will never know the feeling of bounced checks, searching the couch cushions for loose change, or putting two dollars and fifty cents into the gas tank. I, of course, knew all about those things and still experienced them regularly. Guys like Rich won't ever split a cigarette in half at night, saving the rest for the morning. They certainly won't ever break down one rainy morning when they realize they are in some serious financial shit. Most of these people walk around unaware that others can smell their luck, and that it stinks something awful. Richie was one of the few who understood the smell he dragged around with him. But he was comfortable with it. I respected this for whatever reason.

My bedroom had a panoramic view of the Pacific, albeit in the far distance, and I even had my own, spanking new bathroom with obscenely white tiles and a shower twice as large as any I'd ever seen. I had a King bed with fresh sheets and a walk-in closet that I could never fully utilize. I only needed two drawers in the head-high dresser next to the office desk facing the ocean. Most importantly, it was cheap. Richie could have easily gotten twice what I was paying for the space.

And my new good fortune continued. Shortly after moving into Richie's, I got a call from someone named Linda Culbig, an editor at the *Beach Times*, the most popular paper in the South Bay. She apparently had received my online application for a writing gig I saw posted on a website. She wanted me to interview for an open staff writer position. Edward's words had long since lost credibility, but I did agree with his long-ago stated premise that I should work in some capacity as a writer, get my name on the street, as he put it, and this was a great opportunity to do literally that—a byline in a weekly paper sold at newsstands all over the South Bay. This was an area many directors and producers called home, and I was being considered to have my name and my words appear in it on a weekly basis – for pay!

"For starters, I was born in Hermosa Beach and cannot imagine a life away from it," I told Linda.

If it was obvious how full of shit I was, Linda didn't let on.

"And what is it that you love about Hermosa, the Beach Cities?" she asked from her black leather chair on the other side of a huge mahogany desk.

"Well, I just love the fact that I know everyone, everyone knows me. Sometimes you wanna go where everybody knows your name."

Such a ready reference to "Cheers" might have given me away. I thought of how nice a cold beer would taste after Linda finally exposed my lies and I could get on with my day.

"You must have some good, local stories to share with our readers," Linda suggested. "What I need is the insider's take – one of us, talking to us. That's all. A local flare for the details, someone who knows how and where to dig a little deeper into our culture. And it is its own culture, don't you think?"

"It sure is, Linda."

"High school around here?" she asked.

"HB Valley," I said, having passed their street sign minutes prior. Still buying it, somehow.

"College?" she asked, flipping through my mostly-fabricated resume.

"Yup. Loyola Marymount. Student Body President."

"Seems like you have a knack for success and action," she said.

"I try," I said, venturing a little cockiness.

"You're a touch green for the job, Tommy. And by that, I mean that you have literally no experience writing professionally, either as a reporter or otherwise."

Now was as good an opportunity as I would find to write and be read and I didn't want to accept rejection from Linda.

"Experience is not relevant when it comes to writing, Linda. It's about perspective and a unique voice. Let me tell you the Great White story."

"Great White, as in a shark?" she asked.

Her eyebrows raised, a warning to me, I gathered. What I said next would either land me a writing job, or get me laughed out of the *Beach Times*.

"I was only twelve and always trying to get out of my parents' sight. They were crazy-protective, never let me do anything, and can you imagine that in a place like this? All the fun and adventure a kid can get up to in Hermosa, and even at twelve they never let me go anywhere by myself."

"That seems a bit uptight," she said, amusing me.

"You're telling me," I said. "Anyway, one day we're at the beach, my mother watching me like a hawk as always, but I was in the water and they were on the sand, so I drifted out beyond where she was comfortable and pretended I couldn't hear her calling for me to come in. I liked to swim on my own, surf freely, still do. In the water was the only place I ever felt free. Anyway, I'm sitting on my board, you know, waiting for the next set of waves to roll through. Everything is fine and dandy until, all of a sudden, I see a dorsal, just the tip, no more than an inch or two, emerge from the water and pass in front of me."

"A Great White, Tommy?" she asked.

A sudden knot in my gut. But now I was committed.

"So I reached into the water. Inquisitive child, I suppose. My hand brushed across the back of the shark, and he actually looked up and smiled as he passed."

"Then what?" she asked with a half-smile, the kind of look that said she knew I was full of shit, but she was excited to hear it nonetheless.

"Nothing. That's it. He disappeared, off to wherever it is that sharks go. Point is, Linda, if we respect the ocean and its occupants, we will benefit greatly from all it has to offer us. Shoot, that could be the thrust of my first story, don't you think?"

Linda placed my resume on the desk in front of her and lowered her eyeglasses. I couldn't tell if these gestures augured well or ill.

"Next week is the Annual Spring Beach Festival," she said, gazing at me down her nose.

"Of course, it is," I said, as if I had any idea what she was talking about.

"Give me seven hundred words on what it's all about. If you tell me what it's all about, beneath the surface of partying on the Pier and thong bikinis, you'll get a second story. This will be a trial submission, if you will."

"Fantastic."

"And if there is any mention of sharks, or any other fantasy of yours, this first column will be your last."

"Right," I said. I stood up, gathered my things, and got out of Linda's office before she had the good sense to change her mind.

135

I was barely out of the *Beach Times* office before I called Mikey to tell him I was finished waiting tables for him. Sure, my employment at the *Times* was tenuous at best, but it was more than enough for me to give the Stallion the heave-ho.

"Are you fucking kidding me?" Mikey asked.

"I know, right?" I said. "What a fantastic break."

"You couldn't give me five minutes' notice?" Mikey asked.

I explained that the ride up to Westwood from Redondo Beach was not worth my time now that I was a professional writer. At this point, I'd managed to save a few bucks and paid two months' rent in advance, leaving myself broke but now expecting consistent income from the *Beach Times*. This was long-term financial planning by my standards, at this point. No 401K, no health insurance, no dental insurance, no problem.

"Good for you," Mikey said, "but this leaves me in a real jam, Tommy."

For a moment, I almost reconsidered. Mikey was a good sort, all in all, and maybe I could give him a week, at least. But then I remembered what my mother always said about looking out for number one.

"Sorry, Mikey. I'd love to say I'd love to help, but that would be a lie."

I hung up while he was still in the middle of yelling at me.

I stopped by Coffee Bean on Hermosa Avenue for an Americano before hitting the Bank of America on the Hermosa Beach Pier to open a checking account and start my new life of financial independence. I couldn't wait to hit Dad with the news—and not a second too soon. Not only was distant Emily history, but so was passive daydreaming about the life I wanted to live. I was a writer and the first copy of my article that I would send home would prove it. I imagined the sound of pride in Dad's voice as I parked the Pathfinder in Richie's two-car garage and went outside to grab the *Beach Times* on the front doorstep.

The bounce went out of my step, though, when I spotted a bald, gaunt woman gardening next door. I hadn't seen her before now, and she obviously was sick.

"Hi. I'm Tommy," I said, extending my hand. She took it, and her hand felt like it would splinter like bird bones if I applied even the slightest bit of pressure.

"Claudia," she said softly, using her free hand to drag on what smelled like a menthol cigarette. Her t-shirt hung on her like a muumuu, like her shoulders were not shoulders at all, but a coat hanger.

"Nice to meet you. Enjoying the sunshine?" I asked.

"Considering I had a tit removed last week, the sun feels pretty good, yeah."

"Breast cancer?" I asked, as if there was any other reason she would have a mastectomy.

"Yup."

The conversation stalled for a moment as I swayed in my awkwardness. It definitely seemed like I should say something, but I couldn't think of anything that didn't sound impossibly lame in the wake of learning the woman had cancer.

"Everything okay?" I asked finally.

She studied me for an uncomfortable beat.

"My oldest boy is applying to Stanford. My youngest started high school this year."

She ground her smoke into the soil of the garden and a strange smile came across her face, a gripping prelude to the tears forming in her bloodshot eyes.

"How are you feeling? You look a little sore," I said.

"How am I feeling? Looks like I'm dying."

I couldn't think of any appropriate way to respond to that, so instead I blurted out, "I just got my dream job."

She smiled again. "Good for you."

"Jesus, I'm sorry," I said. "That seems pretty inconsequential, given what you're dealing with."

"Not at all. You keep enjoying the sun while it shines, Tommy. I can tell you this ride is a short one. I don't feel a week older than you. Yet here it is, all coming to an end."

"How long?" I asked and braced myself.

"Not sure."

No one had ever told me they were dying, let alone the amount of time they had left to live. I wondered if it was rude that I had asked. I was flailing around, no idea what to say or do, but I tried to focus on how difficult it had to be for Claudia.

"Are you religious?" I asked, sounding just like my mother's son.

"I'm hoping for a late admission to the club," she joked, remind me of my grandmother Jackie in that moment. Jackie found humor when the person around her needed it.

"I'm sure they'll make you an offer."

"I don't have any more answers today than I had yesterday, but it's amazing the things you learn when you're dying. I feel like a one-eyed queen in the land of the blind. I'm just starting to get it and my time is almost up. Of course, those two things are related. If I weren't sick, I'd go on the next thirty years still not getting it."

Ten minutes before I'd been on my way back to the townhouse, intending to call home and tell my parents what a stud they'd raised, how my new writing gig was a clear indication that I'd made the right choice in coming out here, and further that it was merely a pit stop on the road to the ultimate goal, that of being a successful screenwriter. Now, as I hugged Claudia, I was the small creature that God had intended me to be. I could feel the urgency and gratitude in her thin body. It was so real, so honest. She needed it and I needed it. It was beautiful.

I left Claudia and went inside my apartment to call home. My father picked up on the third ring.

"Hey Dad," I said.

"Tommy? How's it going?"

"Mom right there?"

"She is. You want me to put her on?"

"Actually, I want you both on the line. At the same time. If you can manage it."

I told my parents that I loved them, three thousand miles away but as close as ever.

I didn't say anything about the job, or how promising the future looked for me. I didn't mention any of my burdens du jour. Instead, I took my time to relay how much I appreciated them, even if talking about feelings made Dad a little uncomfortable and made Mom choke up. I hung up thinking this was something I didn't do nearly enough, which is surprising because it always felt so great once I had done it.

Not too long ago, Claudia's story would have trapped me in a bad place somewhere in my mind. I would have felt bad for her, bad for me, bad for everyone and everything. I would have seen only the darkness in her being terminally sick, and I wouldn't have felt the warmth and vitality in her embrace. I would have said "fuck it all" and probably gone to the bar to black it all out or lit a joint to numb myself.

But not today. No way.

Richie wasn't a big drinker, particularly after his fall made clear how precious life was, especially a sober and coherent life where he could soak it all in and admire it. Maybe he was onto something. Instead of hitting the town to spend all my money on booze, I went to bed after Richie and I enjoyed a homemade pasta dinner at the dining room table together and joked about how ridiculous we looked. I took it slow, only drinking a small bottle of red wine at dinner and a few beers after we ate.

Barney

Most of the boats had departed Redondo Beach Harbor four or five hours earlier, which I should have known, but luckily I found a tuna boat captain getting a late start, just untying his dock lines when I arrived at 10 am. He seemed like the kind of guy who could tell me something about the area, the kind of deep truth about life in Hermosa Beach that Linda wanted. The 50-ish Captain called himself Barney and he laughed at how I pronounced it.

Barney had leathery skin that could sharpen a sword and blazing eyes a shade of light blue. His grizzly beard led to a strong, wide Superman chin that protruded from below a pronounced underbite. He was obviously a no-nonsense guy, so I told him about my little column and the need to fake my way through it. I'd been full of shit in getting the job, and now I had to be convincingly full of shit to keep it. Barney, who would turn out to be a bit of a yarn-spinner himself, recognized a fellow traveler on the run, and we set out.

"Ever been on a fishing boat?" Barney asked out of the side of his mouth, like a real-life Popeye.

"My old man had a boat, yeah."

"Fishing?"

"We fished a little. Blues and Stripers around the bay, mostly."

"What bay would that be?"

"Duxbury. Marshfield. Great Pines, up to Green Harbor, down to the Cape sometimes."

Barney smiled as he steered the boat. I got the impression he liked my answers, and the fact that I knew a little about fish, but he was so damn tough that he still worried me. I assumed he wouldn't toss me overboard for speaking out of line, but all the same, he had an understated dominance over the situation that was a little unnerving.

"The Chart Room, Falmouth. Great chowder," he said.

"You know the Chart Room?"

"I've been around," he said. I guess so.

For the past few years, I'd held tight to a pessimistic outlook on strangers. For the most part, I hadn't really enjoyed meeting new people, perhaps out of my own insecurities. But if I was to sell a script, or make strides as a human being in general, this would have to change. I thought of meeting Hurst in Cleveland and Claudia in Redondo, even the goth bartender in Hollywood, and decided to open up to Barney more than I normally would.

"Where you from?" I asked as we headed past the last set of channel markers and into open water.

"Charleston."

"South Carolina?"

"That's the one," he said, lighting a smoke and passing it to me.

"You're a long way from home, too."

"This is home, Tommy," he said.

I learned that William Barney was born in Charleston in 1957. His father worked the boats while his mother was a cashier at the local fish market. Uninterested in academia, Barney measured his success on the fish weighing scale at the docks where his dad parked their boat after long outings. Dropping out of school his junior year in high school, Barney took to the seas full-time. Lucky for Barney, one of his father's pals named Harvey Masterson was a sailor and a decent fisherman, too. Masterson had lived his life in preparation for an upcoming world voyage onboard a boat he'd built himself, the 71-foot *Martha Marie*. Barney begged his dad and Harvey for a seat on *Martha Marie* for a world tour. Ultimately, they assented, and Barney would spend his eighteenth birthday somewhere along the African coastline, as his former classmates filed into southern colleges and universities.

After circumnavigating the globe, *Martha Marie* docked in San Diego, California, where she was sold in short order to a local sailor with an abundance of cash at his disposal. Harvey planned to use his cut to return to South Carolina, buy a house, and scheme his next adventure. Barney, on the other hand, met his future wife while on drydock in San Diego and decided to forego the return trip to the east coast. He'd seen the world and decided Southern California was about as good as it gets. Thirty years later, he was the father of three grown boys, all college graduates, and the captain of his own, beautiful fishing vessel. Barney's wife had passed away from colon cancer four years prior, but Barney still talked to her aloud everyday out at sea.

When we got out of land's sight where the boat was in no danger of any type of collision, Barney suggested that I take a turn behind the wheel in the second-level crow's nest as he rigged the fishing lines with bait down below.

"If you're about to hit something, yell to me really loud so I can jump my ass over the side of the boat, you understand?"

"Aye-aye, Captain," I said.

The sun-damaged leather on his face curled into a rock-hard smile.

"Next trip, you're baiting," he said. "Don't get too comfortable in my seat."

"You the man, Barney," I said.

"Bahhnnneeeee!" he wailed, making fun of my accent as he descended the stairs from the crow's nest to the main deck.

"Just drive straight?" I shouted after him, feeling like I needed a little more instruction before I lost him for good.

"Go where it takes you, be aware of what's around you," he hollered from out of sight.

Barney was down below within fifteen feet of me, but I felt alone, and fairly empowered at that atop a large fishing vessel. I watched the hovering seagulls, admired the sun above in the pristine blue sky. I watched the birds swoop and rise above the ocean's surface and my mind began to drift with the waves.

Barney finished baiting the lines, and for the next three hours we trolled increasingly rocky seas. The swells went from four feet to seven feet to nine, and before too long I was puking over the back of Barney's impeccably kept boat.

"I guess," Barney said, "that you don't get this far out in Duxbury Bay."

In between heaves, I confirmed that my father never went out as far or deep as this.

"Sorry," I told him. "I don't normally get sick on boats."

"Don't sweat it," Barney said. "We'll head back and clean this puppy inside and out."

Life to Barney was clearly not about who dies with an arbitrary set of expensive toys, rather who dies the most fulfilled, maybe with that one toy that he really, truly loves. I wondered if he always had this aura about him, or if perhaps the death of his beloved wife afforded him such wonderful perspective. After helping Barney clean the boat from side to side and top to bottom, I left at sunset with an open invitation to join him for a day of fishing whenever I needed it.

As soon as I got home, full with the experience of being out with Barney all day, I got to work on a draft of my first column titled *My Date*:

The Festival is coming. I don't have a date, but that's no matter. Because I came across an old love today, one who is always in my life but too often unappreciated in the rush and bother of the day-to-day.

We live in a true beach community. Any given weekend, we can, if we choose to do so, live a life of sincere gratitude, awed and inspired by the everyday miracle of Redondo Beach. It will take a little effort, but not much. Had a bad day? Head to the water, where it's impossible to stay in a bad mood. Go for a walk in the sand. Watch the children playing, and the terns scurrying along where the waves break.

Or you could just as easily hop a fishing boat and spend the day sportfishing. You can watch dolphins frolic as the sunbeams dance and glisten atop the bluest of blue waters. You can jump in and feel the salt cleanse your skin. You can look to the horizon where blue meets blue, then turn your eyes landward and see your life and all its problems so far away that they might as well not exist.

The best part? You can wake up the next day and do it again, because we all know the temperature will be somewhere between perfect and near perfect. The sun will be shining and the craziness of the rest of the world will remain a safe distance from your beach life. If you can't call in sick, just wait till the weekend. The beach, the waters, and the friendly people will be here come Saturday. The Festival is a celebration of this life on the beach, a life of unknown duration that must be enjoyed. The town we come together to celebrate is my date next weekend. I will dine with her, drink with her, and when the sun goes down and she dons the stars like jewelry, admire her.

Not bad for someone who'd lived in Redondo for less than a month.

****

Spring had always made me horny, especially back home, where when a long and brutal winter finally relented the blood started flowing and everything became quasi-sexual. It's a real thing; look up the science if you don't believe me. And even in California, where the seasons didn't even exist, I felt that same old spring fever to the point where it became torturous and, at times, made me feel like a genuine letch. It was ridiculous. And even though I feared herpes, rancid genital warts, unwanted pregnancy, the big A, and the myriad other horror-show consequences of casual sex, I desperately wanted to screw, because, well, biology rarely gives quarter to good sense. The problem, aside from a complete lack of prospective sexual partners, was that as my column expanded in popularity and word count, I had to spend a significant part of each day on the phone doing research or at my office computer actually writing. Which sucked for two reasons: first, sitting at a desk is not the best or most efficient way to meet women, and two, writing is difficult even under the best of circumstances, but nigh impossible when you're about as focused as a dog in heat.

The single-story office space of the *Beach Times* was unexceptional. About twenty or so cubicles were spread over a brownish-blue carpet beneath bright white lights—the kind designed to encourage productivity at the expense of your eyesight and, eventually, your sanity. My cubicle faced the entrance to our office space so I could always see people coming and going—yet another distraction I didn't need.

I always knew who was taking a cigarette break or sneaking out of the office for a half-day at the beach. It didn't matter to me who was leaving or why, of course, but it was interesting nonetheless watching workers in stealth mode, faking coughs half the morning or offering to bring back coffees like they had any intention of returning—as if anyone was fooled or cared. Most of the people who came into the office were usually there on some sort of professional task, and thus not terribly interesting. They'd drop something off with the receptionist or pick something up from someone in the office. The UPS guy, Frank, was good for a chat but he usually didn't stay long. Aside from that, it was fairly boring. That is, until April 5th at 3:13 p.m.

Up until that day, I couldn't really say I had a "type." Lots of guys I know do, or claim to. There's the time-honored if obvious "ass man," the contrarian who prefers brunettes, and the various light fetishists: those who favor big calves, or gapped teeth, or redheads. Me, I've always been enthusiastic about women in all their iterations. Tall, short, thin or curvy, dark or pale, long hair, short hair, whatever. Then I saw this person, this earth angel floating towards the receptionist amidst the most magnetic aura a human being has ever carried, and I will now forever have a type – shoulder length blonde hair, green eyes, athletic legs, perky breasts, and a subtle yet powerful smile that could've solved California's energy crisis.

She paused at Janelle's desk for a moment as I crept to my feet and peered over the front of my cubicle for a better view. I watched as she reached into a shoulder sack to gather a stack of papers, then handed them to Janelle. I wondered what she was doing here, why she wasn't en route to Paris or Milan for a cover shoot or music video appearance. And you can just forget any kind of perspective. I was already fitting this beauty for a dress and hearing the wedding bells echo off Popponessett Beach back home.

Like one of Barney's fish, I was caught—hook, line and sinker. Now for the difficult part of verbalizing something, anything. One of those moments in life that Mom talked about was here and I wasn't about to let it pass. But there was no time to waste—the woman was already putting her sunglasses back on and turning to go.

As I struggled to find the guts to approach the woman, I noticed Janelle pointing in my direction. I turned to see what was behind me, but somehow the room was empty other than me. Not a single person was at their desk. Maybe there was a birthday party outside and I hadn't been invited. Maybe they had a secret meeting off-site to discuss the imposter amongst them, the man who wrote articles about things he had no real knowledge of. In any event, here came my future wife, floating towards me and removing her sunglasses again. I bobbed up and down in my seat like I was doing speed squats at the gym.

"Are you Willy?" Ms. Millennium Girl Next Door asked as she ran her finger along the top of my cubical. (I had to tell my boss Linda my real name so I could get a paycheck, but we decided to keep the Willy name for the column as the horse was out of the barn).

"No, I'm Tom—yes. Sorry, forgot my name," I said, wanting to punch myself in the face for sounding so stupid.

"I'm Laura Sweeney, head of the Kudos for Kids program. You've heard of us maybe?"

"Absolutely. I admire what you do." No clue, of course.

"The feeling's mutual," she said. "I read your column and I loved it. You do such a great job of capturing the essence of what it's like to live here."

"Thank you," I said, thinking that if I could fool her into thinking I had any idea what I was talking about, maybe I could fool her into wanting to go on a date.

"I'm going around trying to find ways to drum up publicity for our program. I thought your column could help."

"I'd be happy to do whatever I can," I said, "though I usually prefer to help charities in a less public way. I'm not much for people who make a show of how kind and generous they are."

"Oh really?" she said, raising an eyebrow and smiling.

"I'm the church type – church events and charities. Try to 'keep it real' with the homie above."

What on earth are you saying? Shut. Up.

"Jesus is your homie?" she asked. Hearing her repeat what I had said confirmed the worst. I was a total idiot.

"Not quite yet, but I'm tight with some of his disciples."

"Good, so you want to help with my little request?" she asked.

I nodded yes, as I had just decided I would no longer speak – ever again.

"You look busy," she went on. "Why don't we meet for a drink sometime this week?"

Again, I just nodded in agreement.

"Tomorrow good for you? I can tell you about our program and what I hope you can do."

No choice—I had to speak again. "Tomorrow works for me," I said.

"Great," Laura said. "Five o'clock, Good Stuff. See you then."

On the way home from work I stopped at the drug store and bought all sorts of personal care products I never would have imagined spending money on pre-Laura. Lotion, of course, but also overnight acne-fighter, spot-lightening serum, exfoliating cleanser, firming night cream, a few other things I'd never known existed and didn't quite understand the purpose of, other than to make your face look better than it did before you bought them. I didn't know what to do with it all—or whether I should use it all at the same time—but I followed the directions and hoped for the best. In retrospect, going to bed with both the acne fighter and firming cream on was probably a mistake. I woke up in the middle of the night, my face burning as though actually on fire, and when I went to the bathroom and turned on the light my skin was a frightening red, like a bad sunburn. I had until five o'clock the next afternoon—roughly 14 hours—to undo the damage I'd done. I needed to clean up my act.

I rinsed my face for a good ten minutes—no soap, no products of any kind, thank you very much—then went back to bed and draped a cool wet cloth over my face. Several hours later, I got back up and went to the bathroom again, hopeful that the lack of burning meant no permanent damage had been done.

Nothing could have prepared me for what I saw. And in a good way. My face was, in a word, radiant. Some alchemical magic had occurred, and suddenly I had the skin of the Gerber baby. I kind of wanted to have sex with myself. But that would have been neither new nor terribly interesting, so instead I showered, got dressed, applied a liberal dose of lightweight facial oil, and hit the office to show off my new visage.

Work went by in a flash, and I arrived at *Good Stuff* a fashionable two hours before Laura and I had arranged to meet. I skirted past the hostess, grabbed a Bud bottle at the bar, and scoped the joint. I wanted the perfect table, something with a nice ocean view but not a distracting ocean view. I didn't want the ocean to be prettier than me, is what I'm saying. In order to appeal to Laura, I would have to be the main event. I couldn't pass the spotlight to a beautiful sunset, beach joggers, or the whiteness of the delicate sands over yonder. Tonight was *my* night.

By the time Laura arrived, I was half in the bag and had already resolved to a) slow down on the drinking, and b) speak as little as possible.

"You look nice, Mr. Waverider," Laura said, kissing me on the cheek, which was a thrilling surprise.

"Not as nice as you, Ms. Sweeney," I said. So far, so good. "I reserved a table by the window so we can see the ocean."

Laura looked at me kind of strange, and then I remembered she didn't know it was a date just yet.

I decided to run things the way my father would, which is to say I would personally order our drinks and appetizers and look to her for approval as I ordered out of respect. She mentioned a vodka tonic sounded delicious under her breath, so I had a head-start to do the ordering on her behalf.

"The lady will have a vodka tonic, and I will have a Crown Royal on the rocks with a splash," I told the teenage waiter with a horrid mouthful of unfortunate braces. "And could you please bring an order of artichoke dip and some bread?"

A somewhat risky gambit, in an age when some women might get angry at a man for holding a door open for them, but Laura seemed charmed by my effort. In the moment, I remembered that time Emily called me "so rude" for pre-ordering a special $115 bottle of wine on her

21st birthday without her input as to which kind we would be drinking. She scarred me in so many bad ways but the scars were healing well.

Laura looked amazing in a light blue tie-dyed tank top and short white skirt. Her hair was pulled back into a cute ponytail. She was so young and vibrant, and no doubt would be until she died a spunky, lively, strong, bright old woman.

"So, do you need a pen and paper before we start?" she asked.

"I'm an idiot savant, Laura, believe it or not," I said. "Memory of a Dell," I said, tapping my temple.

"Really?" she asked, smiling.

"No. Not really," I said, taking a gulp of Crown. I put my hands on the edge of the table in front of me, elbows locked, and took a deep breath before saying what I had to say. "I am incredibly awed by you, Laura. How's that for an interview topic?"

"Are you hitting on me, Willy?" She looked surprised but not entirely displeased.

"Tommy. My name's Tommy, Laura."

"I thought you were Willy from Redondo."

"The plan is working then, cause I'm about as Californian as a Nor'easter."

"A what?" she asked.

"I'm from Massachusetts, Laura."

Laura sipped her drink and studied the embroidered floral pattern on the napkin in front of her. It seemed several minutes went by, while I imagined she sat there thinking what a fool I was and wondering how she could most easily escape the sudden awkwardness of the scene.

"I don't care," she said suddenly.

"Look, I can leave. Just don't tell anyone."

"No. It's fine. Just, no more lies, okay?" she said, raising a finger to get the attention of the waiter.

"I'm not a liar. I just been doing what I have to do to get . . ."

The waiter showed up.

"Another round," Laura told him, and he scurried away.

Then she turned her gaze back to me.

"I've got four older brothers, it's ok," she said. "They try hard, too."

I sank into my chair as we smiled at each other. The drinks arrived, and we started over.

Laura was not taken. She was not involved. She was not heartbroken from her last asshole of a boyfriend. She was not the mother of a baby girl. Check, check, check. We spent a few drinks discussing her project, which I agreed to promote with a colorful, donation-soliciting column. But neither of us really wanted to talk about that. We found ourselves hungry for information about each other, cautiously bracing ourselves for the other shoe to drop and hoping it wouldn't.

"And Stacy?" she asked in a break in conversation about her younger brother, Mark.

I sat back in my chair and looked out to the ocean. The waves were beautiful, but they were a little more rock and roll than usual.

"She's a little like the ocean current, I guess. If she's against you, don't try to fight it. Accept defeat and guard your nuts."

"Sounds like a strong woman."

"She is. Smart, too. A lawyer at a big-to-do firm. Okay, take for example, the time I helped her move into her apartment in Charlestown."

"Moving," Laura said. "The worst."

"Exactly. She promised to get her friends to help but they hadn't shown up. So I get the call. She promised me a six-pack and a joint, neither of which was anywhere to be found when I arrived. She was pissed that I hadn't got the truck yet, even though I was never told to get any truck. And she was upset that I was fifteen minutes late, even though she changed the meeting time on me twice that day. We argued and argued-

"As brothers and sisters do," Laura interjected. "Believe me, I know."

"Fine. So Stacy gets on the phone and calls my Dad, who is on vacation, to tell him that his son is a good-for-nothing slob who wouldn't help his sister move into her new apartment. Dad called me a 'disappointment,' which was pretty much a reflex for him anyway, and I find myself apologizing to both him and Stacy profusely. At first, I wanted to tell him that I deserved a little respect from the bitch, but he still paid half my bills, mostly through my mother, which he didn't know about, so I didn't want to disrupt that flow of money. That, and if I referred to his daughter as a 'bitch' he would have walked on water from Martha's Vineyard to deliver me a reality check. So I got my buddy, Rob, a big dude I've known forever, and he met me to grab the U-Haul and helped in what Stacy said would be a light move."

"How light are we talking?" Laura asked, starting to giggle.

"Oak. Everything oak. Oversized, unwieldy, from the canopy bed down to the wooden shoe holder things."

"Ouch."

"It took me two weeks to walk straight and three weeks to get a thank-you from Stacy."

"At least she thanked you."

"Oh, she thanked me. She sent me two hundred bucks, a gift certificate for dinner at Flemming's, and threw in a bag of weed worth another hundred. Rob got the same care package."

"Interesting."

"Yes, very. And that's how it goes with Stacy. Tough to tell what you're gonna get sometimes."

"But she'd do it for you."

"Huh?"

"Stacy. If you had to move in a pinch, she'd be there in a heartbeat, wouldn't she? She'd be there for you, I bet."

"Probably."

"That's what matters."

"I like the way you think," I said.

"I like the way you talk," she said.

As it turns out, Laura's dad was an enforcer and her mom was a pint-sized almanac just like mine. Her brother Mark had a habit of threatening her boyfriends' lives only because he loved her so much. The only major difference between us, as far as we could tell at this point, was that she had animals and I didn't. I always wanted a golden retriever but my pleas fell upon deaf ears because we had marsh behind our house and there was no way my mother was cleaning marsh mud off the floors every time there was a low tide. Laura didn't live around marsh, though, and was granted Percy, a black and white sheep dog, and Gorda, a little cat that looked like a miniature tiger and ate like one, too. We laughed and talked our way from Good Stuff, made a stop for ice cream cones, went to Richie's pad, took a quick tour, and then, just as casually and happily as you like, heaved ourselves into my un-made bed.

Two used condoms and two near-death kids sweating in the bed said it all. I usually spurn the post-sex cuddling and small talk for a tall glass of water, a cigarette, or the comforts of digging my face into a cold pillow, refusing all forms of communication. Not with Laura, though. I wanted to enjoy every second of her, every inch of her until I would have to fall asleep against my will. If I could, I would have stayed awake all night to marvel at her soft eyes and dimples and run my fingers up and down every inch of her soft, tanned skin.

"Why did you move to California?" she asked.

"Long story."

"You don't have to tell me the whole thing."

I thought for a moment. "I was tired of myself," I said finally.

"What does that mean, exactly?"

"It means, I guess, that I could have easily stayed in Boston and become some version of the guy everyone, myself included, expected me to be. Work some middle-management job, marry the first girl who'd have me, spend the rest of my life on a trajectory towards a heart attack."

"Is selling a movie script what you have to do to prove yourself?" Laura asked.

I rolled over onto her and tucked her hair behind her ears. "I have no idea," I said. "All I know is I was so claustrophobic to live a life that was dictated by someone other than me. Or by the accident of where I was born. Or by the fact that my old man was a cop, and there was a certain set of possibilities that went along with being a cop's kid. So on and so on. So many of the people I know seem perfectly comfortable living the lives that were more or less handed to them at birth, graduating, moving into a sterile McMansion in Hingham when they make their bones at Fidelity Investments or whatever. Thinking about that made me depressed, and when I tried to accept it and live with it, it made me insane. Does that make any sense?"

She had no idea what most of these references were, but she listened, anyway.

"You need space to roam. Who doesn't?" she said and kissed my neck.

"Exactly. A little control, a little creativity. That's why it's not about selling a script. It's more about leading a life I want to live, which just so happens to be in front of a computer, writing."

"Are you in control now of this life of yours?" she asked.

"Getting there," I said, and realized, to my surprise, that I meant it..

"Good. Although sometimes we have to relinquish control."

"What does that mean?" I asked.

But she didn't respond. Instead, she smiled and pulled the covers over   our   heads.

158

All in a Day

One day not too long after that first glorious night with Laura, I was running on the Hermosa Beach Strand, having passed the party girls on the roof deck at Hennessey's and the ever-present posse of oiled, bikini-bottomed men who drank Zima's on a beachfront porch on 26th Street, when I noticed something odd on the horizon. In the near distance I could see that a production team had quarantined a house on the Strand and set up a lavish spread of lights, cameras, and action. As I drew closer, I could see there must have been a hundred people buzzing around the set, adjusting lights, plugging in electrical cords, and making sure the next shot would be in line with the director's vision. Everyone was so professional with their little clipboards, headphones, and walkie-talkies. I couldn't help but stop my run and watch a movie being created.

I wanted to barge onto the set and begin interrogating everyone I could get my hands on. *What's your job here? Who wrote the script? Who's the director? Any stars I'd know? How much does all this stuff cost? Do you rent this equipment or what?* I wanted them to tell me about their days on the set, the ups and downs of movie creation. I wanted to know how they came to be where they are today – in the heart of a creative process. The set was ringed by orange traffic cones and a few private security guards. I knew this must involve some important people who demanded people like me be kept at a safe distance. At first glance, I couldn't devise a plan to get on the inside. Every possible point of entry was guarded by unsmiling men, and while they were each about as intimidating as the average mall cop, just the fact of their presence would make getting onto the set difficult. They really did their homework on the security front and I would have to be crafty to overcome their precautions.

The set was constructed on the back door of a mansion facing the Strand and the beach. A large overhang had been mounted onto the back of the house, either for lighting or privacy reasons, perhaps both. Inside this overhang was where the good stuff was being hidden. The directors, producers, and actors, and the actual, moment to moment, scene to scene act of creating a film. Inside that tented area was where the magic happened and I could not be denied admission to this party. I nestled myself up to a security guard, a 20-ish kid straight out of Dogtown with more interest in the surf crashing into the sand than the movie behind him, and tried to make some small talk. He was paid a good wage to stand there and make sure no one attacked the property or persons of the movie, but surely there was nothing in his contract against mingling with the onlookers.

"Need a break?" I asked him.

"Huh?" he said, with a lip curl that suggested he was high or upset.

"I can take it from here, man," I said. "You know the union rules as well as I do. Fifteen minute break every two hours, an hour break every six. You're due, brother."

"You Production?" he asked, still crunched up around the nose like something smelled funny.

"That's me," I said and pretended to search for a badge or identity card of some sort in my back pocket.

And can you believe it? He actually bit.

"Hell yeah, bra. My board's in my car. Right on," he said and skirted off like a thief looking over his shoulder.

And with that, I was on the inside. I grabbed a seat on one of the plastic folding chairs facing the director and tried my best to keep from drawing anyone's attention. I was clearly out of place, but then I realized these people were entirely too busy to question me. They all had very specific job descriptions that had nothing to do with noticing whether or not someone belonged on the set. That had been surfer dude's very specific job description, and he'd abandoned his post. Emboldened by this realization, I raised my head and looked around a bit, and that was when I saw a clapperboard emblazoned with the name of the production I'd crashed: Charlie's Angels II.

Then things got exceptionally weird.

Cameron Diaz took a seat next to me in a folding chair to enjoy a bottle of Evian. As Stacy might say, *ohmifrikkingawd*! This woman somehow melded the striking beauty of a runway model with the cuteness of a high school sweetheart. There *was* something about Mary, particularly in person. I couldn't utter a word if my life hung in the balance. The sights and sounds of her muted me. This was definitely the first time I have ever marveled at the way someone's throat sounded when they drank water. Then, to make matters a little more interesting, out of the house came Drew Barrymore, Matt Leblanc, Lucy Liu, Luke Wilson, and Bernie Mac. One by one, they took seats around Cameron – and me. I was in a mess, suddenly, and I knew it. No way I was going to continue to fly under the radar with every star of the film seated around me.

I was frozen in time, a very awkward and embarrassing time at that. This was so much worse than the dreams I had been having recently about public masturbation. For a brief instant I envisioned pulling the director's t-shirt over his head a la P.J. Stock and whaling him senseless to create a diversion before running, but that vision faded to reality quickly.

"I'm a writer for *The Hollywood Reporter*," I submitted for all to scrutinize and attack.

"Max?" Luke Wilson asked. I couldn't tell if he was serious or throwing me a bone.

"That's me," I said, turning to him with a smile. I offered my hand, and he took it.

"Bev said we were meeting later on today," Luke said. Still couldn't tell if he was acting or not.

"We are, yes," I told him. "But I was hoping I could just sort of lurk around the set a bit, get a feel for what's going on for the story."

Luke looked over to the director, eyebrows raised with approval.

"Fine," the director said. "Just don't get in the way."

I got off the chair, making way for the director, and stood off to the side while they ran lines for the next scene. Ten minutes later, when they set the scene up and got ready to shoot, I still somehow hadn't been thrown out.

I watched them roll cameras once, twice, a dozen times. I watched Luke flub his lines repeatedly. I watched peons adjust lighting time and again, and each time I couldn't for the life of me tell what the difference was. I watched several boom mics gets swapped out until the sound guy (identifiable by the gigantic seventies-style headphones clamped over his ears) indicated, with a hearty thumbs-up, that they were getting exactly the quality and levels needed to do justice to the scene.

The whole time, an hour or more, I felt a weird, sinking feeling. I couldn't quite put my finger on what it was, at least not at first. What I could identify was that my ass had started to numb from just sitting there, and I found myself distracted by the most mundane things—the sound of a police siren passing on the street outside, for example, or the artful arrangement of a fruit plate on the craft services table. My mind wandered: to Laura, to that week's column for the *Beach Times*, which I'd had yet to start or even conceive a topic for. As the director and stars blocked out the scene for the umpteenth time and some guy who looked unnervingly like a rat slammed a clapperboard yet again, I realized, finally, what was going on: I was *bored*.

As bored as I'd been sitting in church at age 11. As bored as I'd been every day at the shitty job I'd had before leaving Boston. Was this what I wanted? Was *this* my dream? Sweating blood as I wrote lines that a bunch of over-exercised, self-important people would mangle time and again? Playing the world's dullest game of make-believe? This was what I wanted?

But I wasn't an actor, and I wasn't a director. I was a *writer*. I didn't have to sit through watching the sausage get made. I got to write the sausage, and I got to see it when it was finished. But this—all this drudgery and stupidity—I would be spared, for the most part. In other words, I had the best job in Hollywood. I just had to convince someone to give me a shot.

And that was when the real Max, who was really a writer for the *Hollywood Reporter,* showed up. All eyes turned to me as Max introduced himself to the cast and crew that were taking another break in their seats. Sometimes there are no words, and this was one of those times. I simply stood up, dusted the sand off my chair with my hand, and walked away. Aaaaaand...scene.

I heard them all giggle as I tripped over an equipment chest of some sort before officially being outside their set limits. But, in what was nearly an epically embarrassing moment, I had come out completely satisfied. And with a killer story that no one is going to believe. Ever.

****

"Good run, honey?" Claudia asked from her garden, looking as sick as ever.

"Not bad at all. Getting my legs back," I said and walked over to help her haul the full wheel barrel of weeds and trimmings to the screened-in compost pile adjacent to her garden.

"My sons have backs like yours," she said.

Placing the empty wheel barrel to the ground, I put my arm on her shoulders and looked into her eyes. She looked like a little girl.

"Just look how strong their mom is," I said.

Claudia's head dropped momentarily before reassuming teary eye contact with me.

"It's over, Tommy."

"What's over?", I asked but knew what was over.

"It's over. I did my best."

"I don't understand," I said but, again, I understood.

She looked at me, almost pityingly. "You know, there are some people who think the last great frontier is actually inside us. There's nothing left of the world to map, Tommy. And we've set foot on the moon. But inside us is still a big mystery."

"That's all really interesting, Claudia, but I still don't understand what it means."

She sighed. "Sorry. It's the sort of thing that suddenly seems really profound when you know your time's almost up. Anyway, my insides got a little less mysterious yesterday, thanks to the latest CAT scan. Cancer's spread to my liver. I'm finished. I have two months, maybe."

I certainly couldn't think of a damn thing to say about that, so instead I just reached out my arms and wrapped them around Claudia's thin shoulders. It felt so odd to hug a woman who I knew would be dead soon.

"The funeral's been arranged," she said.

"It's not fair."

"*Life*. It's not fair, but it's here in front of you, isn't it?"

"I'll bring you flowers from this garden every day."

"I won't be there, sweetie. As soon as I pass through, I'm gone, Tommy," she said.

"Where are you going?" I asked.

"My body hurts. As soon as I get my wings back, I'm going to fly until they break. I'll be around, but not under a headstone."

"You're an amazing woman, Claudia."

"Thank you, Tommy. I hope I've taught my boys a thing or two, the important stuff."

"I can just about guarantee that," I said.

I watched Claudia for a few minutes and she let me stand there and watch, not forcing conversation with me. I find it hard to describe those bonds we have with certain people where voids created – by silence or distance or time – don't need to be explained or filled.

Shit Outta Luck

Kudos For Kids had a nice little setup on the ground floor of an industrial park, with an ocean view for most classrooms and a large lawn outside designated for playing and mingling. Laura said there was something about the vitamin D in the sun that was good for the kids' spirits, and I told her my own experience confirmed that. I was running four or five miles a day on the Strand and I had never felt better: my back was straight, my vision acute, my mind clear and sharp. Claudia's condition had motivated me to get healthy and exercise had a way of pumping up my endorphins and positivity. I popped out of bed in the morning, and had enough energy to do my day job and work on my screenplay most every day. The exercise was good for me, sure, but I'd become convinced that the real benefit was from the sunlight. Yet another way in which California was better for me than Boston.

I'd come to Kudos for Kids to do research for my column, and when these 'special' kids hit the exit doors for recess, nothing seemed terribly special about them to me at first. They flew out the doors just like normal kids do at normal schools. With huge smiles and plans for a visit with friends and love interests outside the building's constraints, they bowled over anything and everything in their paths to get to the prearranged meeting point to shoot the shit or pick daisies with classmates. Laura and I followed the raging herd of kids out the doors for a closer look to aid me in writing an accurate summation of her program for the *Beach Times*.

"Watch Samuel," Laura said, "He's my favorite." Laura pointed to a chubby twelve-year-old with Down's Syndrome sitting alone in the shade in the far corner of the lot under a tree.

"What's his deal?"

"He doesn't have a deal, Tommy. He's just Samuel."

"Sorry."

"Don't be. You just have to remember that these kids are people. That sounds obvious, probably, but too often they're looked at as problems to be solved, or managed. Or worse, avoided."

As usual, Laura had a way of framing things that made me feel like I'd just taken a master class in how to be a decent human.

"Does he want to be alone?" I asked.

"Not more than me or you. He struggles with anger, which makes it more comfortable for him to be alone, sometimes. But he's still lonely. When he's ready to talk, he will. He's happy playing with the bugs and the leaves that fall from that tree."

"You don't think you should talk to him, coddle him?"

"Naw."

"I would think he'd want the company. Loneliness blows."

"He likes to be alone sometimes and watch it all from a distance. Maybe he doesn't need attention like everyone else."

Maybe she was right. Maybe Samuel liked to be alone, though I doubted it. I wanted to go over and hug him, but Laura said to just leave him be. And she was the expert. Still, it seemed sad to me, all the other kids screaming in joy and running in circles and falling in love and enjoying the sunshine, while Samuel sat cross-legged and alone in the shade. When Laura headed to the food table, I took the opportunity to make a new friend.

"Samuel?" I said, taking a knee next to him under the shade of the tree.

I must say, his spot was great. Good view. Comfy temperature. Soft soil. Cool array of bugs. Samuel's tongue was flopped between his teeth and protruded out from his lips. He seemed underwhelmed by my arrival. In fact, he didn't even bother to look up, and I felt immediately out of my depth, unsure if I should keep talking, wondering if it would have been smarter to heed Laura's advice and leave him alone.

"Samuel, I'm Tommy, nice to meet you," I said. "Nice place you've got here. Can I get the name of your realtor?"

He bobbed his head up and down a few times quickly but still didn't speak.

"Laura's great, isn't she?" I asked.

He bobbed some more, this time with a smile like Laura's name gave him secret pleasure.

"Boyfriend?" he asked.

"Yes, boyfriend," I said, "*You* have girlfriend?"

"Laura," he said.

"Yes, Laura is my girlfriend," I confirmed.

169

"No, *my* girlfriend, stupid," he stated, and shook in wild laughter.

I couldn't help but join him.

"Okay, pal, I'll share her for a little while, but I think you can get your own girl, don't you?"

He shrugged and went back to licking his lips and petting the baby caterpillar on his wrist.

I watched the other boys flirting with the girls and the counselors monitoring the action to make sure no one was being hurt or hurting others. There were a couple of minor dustups, as will happen when kids, "special" or otherwise, are cut loose to form their own associations and rules. But for the most part the students seemed to know exactly how to let it all hang out without any regard for coolness or outside judgment. What most people wouldn't give to run around and smile so wildly, to live with such an utter and sincere lack of self-consciousness.

"You don't want to play grabass with the girls over there?" I asked Samuel. "You know, I'd appreciate if you stop your affair with my lady."

Samuel hucked the caterpillar against the tree and didn't answer me immediately. He certainly played like he was content to be alone, but I hoped it wasn't just a front to give that impression. I knew how exhausting that could be. I'd been playing that game, offering the world inauthentic versions of myself, for most of my life.

"I play with my friends here," he said finally, dangling a rather large spider by its leg. I had the feeling that for Samuel, these bugs were not unlike my *Boston Herald* sports page, or a medium Dunkin Donuts French Vanilla coffee.

After half an hour or so it was time to pile back into the classroom for roll call to make sure no one had drifted into traffic during recess. Laura wasn't teaching her next class for another forty-five minutes, so we grabbed a seat on the lawn and tore through some peanut butter and jelly sandwiches.

"How did it go with your new friend?" she asked.

"You didn't tell me you were cheating on me."

"*Oh, no.* He told you?"

"How do you do it, Laura?"

"What?"

"Change a fifteen-year old's diaper. It's not even your child. Where do you get the energy to break up a fight between two grown, strong boys with the mental capacities of three-year-olds?"

"It's nothing. Anyone can do it."

"No, Laura. I certainly can't. I used to wonder the same thing about my mom, all moms. How do they do it? How do they wake up in the morning and say, 'I'll spend the next fifteen hours of my life making sure everyone else is happy'? How can you live so unselfishly? I don't get it."

"It's easy. Find something you love and love it. It's all a privilege. I get more out of it than you think."

"And that's my point," I told her. "The fact that you get more out of it than you put in is what makes you special. Not everyone is that way. Not everyone is that good."

I looked out to the ocean, which was a little too far away to put into clear focus, and wondered how Barney was doing with the tuna. I knew he was somewhere out there talking with his wife and thinking about how great his three kids and big boat were. In a few hours, he'd return to the harbor to scrub the decks and clean his fishing rods meticulously. I smiled at the thought and took a bite of a soggy graham cracker.

"I'm gonna fall in love with you, Tommy," my angel said softly into my ear, filling my heart to its brink.

What a day.

****

"Tommy, my man," Edward said, "Your ship has come in."

As much as Edward's sleaziness made me want to shower, it was actually a fantastic feeling to hear his voice. It had been months since we'd last spoken and I was really starting to wonder if my time had passed, if my screenplay sucked, if I was going to be a weekly paper columnist forever.

"What ship?" I said, still a little groggy from the last night's rare booze fest with Richie and Laura down at the Pier.

"Arnold Goldberg wants to chat with you about 'Dreams Come True'," Edward said, barely containing himself.

"Arnold *who*?" I asked.

"Tommy!" he blurted, "Arnold is only the top coming-of-age producer the last ten years."

"And by coming-of-age you mean teen movie?"

"You say that like it's a bad thing. Teenagers buy movie tickets, Tommy. Lots of them."

"I didn't write a kids' story."

"You did if Arnold Goldberg says you did."

"I don't know, Edward..."

"Tommy, don't be a fool."

"How's your assistant Katrina doing, man?" I don't know why, I just felt like busting this guy's balls a little.

"Katrina? I fired her, why?"

"What's the new girl's name?"

"Unique."

"Yeah? What is it?"

"That's it. Unique. Look, we need—"

"Valley stripper?" I had to ask.

"Tommy, you're wasting my time."

"Ed," I said, sitting up on my couch in my boxers as I looked for my glasses, "you know I want nothing more than to sell a script, but aren't we fooling ourselves to think a guy like Arnold Goldberg will front the cash for a low budget, edgy script about synchronous dreaming patterns? It's too out there, too risky."

"That's for him to decide, Tommy, not you. Rule number one in Hollywood: if someone's interested in giving you money, you don't tell them why they shouldn't. Arnold called me back personally, Tommy. I sent him the script blind and he called us back. Now is not the time for second-guessing. Remember, it only takes one movie deal from one studio to make you a very rich man. Should I confirm the meeting or not?"

I rested my head against the arm of the couch and stared at the ceiling, stalling, trying to think. I wanted to see the story I wrote told onscreen. I also wanted to see my name scroll across that same screen for the whole world to admire. The problem was I wanted these things too badly. I knew a meeting with Arnold Goldberg would turn into him telling me what was wrong with my script, citing its graphic detail that most audiences aren't ready or willing to view. And I knew the meeting with Arnold would probably end once he realized that he had made a mistake with me and my script. But I had to hear it for myself.

"Set the meeting," I said.

So I took the bait, hungry and a little desperate, and went forward with all the necessary preparations for my meeting with Mr. Arnold Goldberg. For all I knew, this Arnold character shared an office with Cherrie the Fake, but the thought of him optioning "Dream Come True" gave me the necessary motivation I needed to prepare. With only a day and a half notice, I was pressed for time, but this may very well have been a good thing. That way I didn't have too much time to ponder how things might implode on the way to, or during, the meeting.

The day before my meeting at Warner Brothers, I pulled up some directions from Mapquest and made a quick trip to the gas station to fill up the tank of the Pathfinder. I still had a full day to prepare but I liked to get these types of crucial things I would usually forget out of the way. I wanted to spend the day of the meeting concentrating on my material, not on trying desperately to find a gas station off the 405 when I was running late and on empty. The rest of the day I spent jogging on the Strand, organizing some paperwork I would bring to my meeting, and sleeping like a baby. I felt oddly comfortable and at ease. There wasn't too much this town could throw at me I haven't already seen or heard about, and I was beginning to act like it.

I woke up the day of the meeting and had a bowl of cereal with a sliced banana on top. I usually had a glass of orange juice, too, but I had run out yesterday and forgot to pick some up at the store. A glass of cold water did the trick, followed by a strong cup of home brewed coffee with a few scoops of sugar and some half 'n half. Rich was long gone to his workplace (he got up at an ungodly hour that I'd never pinpointed), so I had the house to myself to prepare for the next couple of hours before I departed for Burbank. After a long, hot shower I dressed myself in a fashionable suit that Laura had bought me to replace my itchy wool sports jacket. I slicked my hair back like the hot shot I was. I felt remarkable for a non-morning person. I looked great, smelled great, and my mind was incredibly clear.

The key to a successful pitch, I'd come to assume, was to stop worrying about what I could take from the table, what I stood to gain. Of course, it was impossible to put that out of my mind completely, but what I really had to be thinking about, if I wanted to make the sale, was what I could tangibly *bring* to the table. That's what these guys wanted to hear. It wasn't about me. It was about them. In an exec's mind, my only plausible role was to help make them look more genius. To do so, I had to talk not just like an artist, but like a businessman, like someone who was aware of and understood the different things that constituted a movie's bottom line. I had to talk about things like marketability and target audience, and what might constitute a box office success. Detailing the actual script, the plots and subplots and character bios, was the introductory pitch, but the real *sale* went beyond the story and into the realm of dollars and cents. And in the room, this happened very quickly. One moment you were going on and on about your protagonist and his arc through the story, and the next thing you knew the air pressure had changed, the temperature had gone up twenty degrees, and you were fielding questions about shooting budgets and whether the script you'd written would require a second unit. It was all about "the next big thing," according to Edward, and I had to somehow convince them that my script and I were just that. I was the last flight to paradise. They could catch me or not. With or without them, I was on my way to coladas and string bikinis.

I gave myself plenty of time to go up the 405, cross the 101 and the 134, and make it to Burbank. I usually listened to something heavy metal or rap-oriented to pump me up for these meetings, but so far that strategy had yielded nothing but disappointment. So today I went with an old Taj Mahal CD that Uncle Bill had bought me years earlier, at a time when I was listening to Marky Mark and breakdancing on a piece of cardboard smeared in Crisco for the neighbors. Uncle Bill said I would appreciate it someday, and it turned out he was right. The sound of Taj Mahal jamming about catching catfish and losing his fine woman and enjoying drunken days on a Southern porch kept me cool. My mood stayed very relaxed all the way through Santa Monica and onto the 101 heading east.

I should have known the other shoe was about to drop.

Something had to go wrong, as it always seemed to for me. So maybe I wasn't *entirely* surprised when, a minute or so from the Warner lot with plenty of time to spare, I felt an ominous rumble in my gut and realized in short order that I was about to shit my pants.

And it wasn't going to stop there if it started. I would destroy every article of clothing I had on me, from my socks to my watch. It was either squeeze my ass cheeks as hard as humanly possibly or miss my meeting at Warner Bros. I have never actually shit my pants, aside from the time I *slightly* soiled my boxers on the way to the movies two summers before. That particular night, what I thought was a fart was not a fart at all. I don't count that time, though, because it was more of a manageable accident than a day-wrecking disaster. What I had on my hands on this particular day was something much, much worse, something from the feel of it, more akin to dysentery.

And then, of course, I hit traffic. Cars stopped on all sides of me. I was in the middle lane of a five-laner and starting to sweat like I was doing sit-ups in a hot sauna. I couldn't even switch a lane, let alone get off the highway and find a bathroom to paint. The phone rang as I fought off disaster with everything I had. I wasn't even sitting on my seat anymore. I was standing on the brake pedal of the Pathfinder, clutching and gripping the wheel with all my might.

"Hello," I said, out of breath.

"Tommy, you okay?" asked Stacey.

"Stace, I can't talk. I'm in big trouble."

"What's the matter?" she asked, concerned.

I grunted and cupped the seat of my pants with my right hand. "I'm stuck in traffic and I'm about to shit myself."

A pause.

And then, Stace laughed and laughed, sounding like a hyena with a megaphone. Though I knew it would result in disaster, I couldn't help myself—I started laughing, too.

"Stace," I said, in between guffaws, "you gotta stop. I'm really going to shit my pants."

This, of course, only made her laugh harder. So I laughed harder. And then it all let go.

Stacey hung up, not wanting to bear witness to my shame, even over the phone. And so I sat there in my ruined suit that Laura bought me, traffic still at a standstill, and finished filling my pants. All pride and self-regard were gone, as well as any chance of making the meeting. No use fighting it now.

Certainly I was not the first person to shit themselves on the 405. And I probably was not the last. I would guess, though, that I am the first aspiring screenwriter who has missed an appointment at Warner Brothers because I shit my pants en route.

Within seconds of soiling my future, the car accident ahead instantly cleared up and allowed me the opportunity to turn around and head home for a shower. But that was the booby prize. Edward understood my need to no-show as best he could and wished me a quick clean up after we had clarified the circumstances and how shit happened. It was totally unnecessary to tell him the truth, but I figured what the fuck. Once you've sat in your own excrement for the better part of an hour, there's not much pride left, and not much embarrassment in having to tell the story. Besides, the truth, in this case, was utterly convincing, because why would someone lie about that?

Arnold Goldberg reconsidered his initial opinion of my script that same day and thanked me, via Edward, for making the effort despite my emergency peptic ulcer surgery. He, too, wished me a speedy recovery. There was no need for me to reschedule at this time, Goldberg said. Time is of the essence in Hollywood and, dysentery or not, you don't stand up a man like Mr. Goldberg and expect a second go-round. I could think of a million reasons why there was a need to reschedule personally, but what I thought didn't matter.

I'd missed my chance and shit myself like a three-year-old to boot, but strangely enough, I felt fine. Better than fine, in fact—I felt relaxed and happy and content to know that the world would offer more opportunities, that Arnold Goldberg was not the only producer in the sea, and that my whole life didn't hinge on the meeting that wasn't. This was just one more ridiculous event in a life full of them, and besides, I was in love. I couldn't wait to for Laura to get off work so I could tell her what had happened, secure in the knowledge that, despite how disgusting a day I'd had, she would still love me nonetheless—would, in fact, probably love me even more for making her laugh.

Fridge Art

I didn't recognize the number, but I picked up anyway.

"I enjoyed your column, Willy, but I must express some concern about it if I may," the voice said on the phone.

"And you are?" I asked.

"A reader."

"Ok, a reader, thanks for reaching out," I said, preoccupied with a tense game of tic-tac-toe against myself on a notepad at my desk.

"You see, Willy, you made me laugh. And dashboard-pounding traffic in L.A. deserves a stroke of humor across it."

"So what's the problem? I'm busy here," I said, about to lose to X's.

"The problem is this, Willy. How can a young man who has lived here for such a short time period hold such strong convictions about this issue, any local issue, really? You're funny, Tommy Rafferty, I'll give you that, but you're also about as Californian as Jimmy Carter. Tell me, Tom, how long has this charade been going on?"

I dropped my pencil. So that was it. The jig was up. Willy the Waverider was busted. I sat there, stunned into silence, still holding the phone to my ear. And then I heard, on the other end, a cackle, a fit of wet tubercular coughing, and a now-familiar voice saying, "Lord Jesus, Tommy, you're a gullible one." Barney. The bastard.

"Well, sir, I do appreciate your feedback. I don't know anything about fishing, either, so perhaps you'll like next week's article."

"Is that right?" Barney asked.

"Yes, I think you will, in fact. I'll be discussing the best kept secrets of the local fishing world, the undiscovered hotspots an old prick once showed me."

More cackling and coughing.

"Aren't you worried what this old prick will do when he gets his hands around your neck?"

"There'll be a map, too, to avoid any conceivable chance of confusing the novice angler."

"Ha," Barney cackled, done with his joke. "How are ya, Tommy?"

"Good, Barney, thanks. Yourself?"

"How about some fishing, you and me, kid?"

"Tell me when and where and I'm there, man."

"Tomorrow. Four-thirty on the docks."

"Great, I'll see you at seven?"

"Not a minute later, Rafferty."

But I was 'later'. By a lot. Not my fault, I told Barney—the barista at Coffee Bean had gotten my order wrong again. Twice.

"And that took an extra half-hour?" Barney asked.

"It's a complicated order," I said. "Takes time to get it right."

The fish weren't biting. Barney blamed our late departure, which meant he blamed me. It was too hot to catch fish, he said. I reminded him how well we did the first time out at midday, and he reminded me not to speak about things of which I had no business speaking. Maybe I missed tormenting my Dad and needed to give Barney a few headaches to fill the gap in my life of disappointing male authority figures.

"This is the last time you're late for fishing with this Captain," Barney said.

But hope sprang eternal, at least for me. Every once in awhile our bait would hit a current, or a line would catch a gust of wind, and the rod would bend slightly, causing me to jump from my seat as Barney just sat and smirked. I should've known these baby rod bends were not the same as when a tuna realized he had a hook in his mouth and a date with a Starkist packaging plant and started to really throw some weight. After a while even I clued into the fact that getting scrappy with a hell-bent tuna was not in the cards, and we just drifted along and nursed Tecates in the sun. We were both blitzed halfway through the twelve-pack that Barney kept cold in a secret icebox in the cabin for when the fishing faltered.

A few weeks before I'd asked just about everyone that I knew who was older than me to write a short essay about where they were in life at my age. Barney had yet to complete his *When I Was Twenty-Five* assignment and I doubted he ever would, but I read aloud to him the submission I got from Stacy, who always had a remarkable way with words:

Hey Tommy,

THE MAKING OF TOMMY RAFFERTY

I was always a greater version of myself on my own, outside our family. Sorry, but it's true. I watched how everyone else lived and started to bring together an understanding of how my life could be conducted through the best of all I encountered. My friends, these exceptional people full of heart and intellect, they hosted the unraveling of a young girl, never having known herself. Graduating high school, my life surfaced bearing transcendent ardency. Although struggle inevitably weaves together moments mounting toward accomplishment, opportunities seemed to present themselves easily, as if in capsules waiting for time to burst them open. A course of benchmarks.

I am on the doorstep of today. And I remember thinking in the back of my mind that I would never make it because I couldn't imagine myself here. I understand why. For a young lifetime, progress, on a daily basis built in. It is called education. Going to school, doing homework — student- that is the role a young person fills. There is no need to prove yourself otherwise. Goals are set and you work toward them in a community of peers. Graduate. Suddenly, without really knowing it, you are left to build a mold of worthwhile existence to fill, built of you own materials; the intangibles strengthened and nurtured by your education. The very grain of self-worth is progress and relentless self-criticism is what drives me, fumbling, towards this understanding. My uncertainty lies in something greater that the frustrated version of myself. We are caught in a breath of evolution.

But survival of the fittest is no longer defined by perpetuation of the species or physical strength. Fitness of the mind, this remains the last frontier. Boredom and restlessness will destroy those who do not seek to constantly construct, to procreate, mentally as opposed to physically. Soft and light, relief as an adult is simply the promise of delayed gratification. But I am not alarmed. My vision remains strong. I don't want time to be the only thing that separates me today from what I was a year ago, two years ago.

These are our "making of" years, and we go through them together.
Love, Stacy

The 'making of years', I liked that.

I wasn't smart enough to understand everything Stacy wrote, but I still felt like I knew her better when I read her words. It sounded to me like I wasn't the only one standing on uneasy legs on the doorstep of the future. I thought Barney could help me figure it out. I put Stacy's papers down in my lap and waited for a response from Barney, but he just stared out at the water and took a swig of his beer, as if he hadn't heard a word of it.

"Well?" I asked.

"Well, what?" he said, swiveling slowly in the captain's chair.

"What do you think?"

"You kids think too much today. That's what I think."

"Huh?"

"Ride the waves a little, Tommy, relax."

Barney's words often had two levels. At first, I heard the obvious meaning, the one everyone hears, but then, if I thought hard enough about it, I could catch the more subliminal, or intellectual message.

"See, your generation thinks we've got it made – no draft, no depression, no Cold War," I said.

"That's right."

"Can you imagine the amount of pressure that puts on kids today? The assumption is that our parents and grandparents have done all the legwork, baby-boomed, and the rest is gravy. It's not."

"We did do some legwork, Tommy, and we . . ."

"And what about Iraq and Afghanistan and red and green and yellow terror alerts? And competition for . . ."

"I'll be back," Barney said, taking the last swill of his beer before heading into the cabin, seemingly uninterested in my pseudo-hippie speak. Seconds later, though, he reemerged.

"Just one thing, Tommy," he said, flipping me a full Tecate. "If you know all this pressure is a crock of shit, misplaced, something an unfair world has bestowed upon an entire generation, mostly on *you*, something you couldn't *possibly* control, then why do you let it get to you?"

The easy answer, my well-rehearsed answer, was that that this world was a hamster wheel, without meaning or direction. It was precisely *because* we had no great challenges—no Great Depression, No Cold War—that we lacked anima and purpose. I was about to say all this and more to Barney, and then I heard it in my head and realized it sounded to me, now, exactly how it sounded to Barney: like whiny bullshit.

"Maybe you're right," I said, finally.

"Maybe. Maybe not. You're smarter than me."

And then, as if on cue, one of the rods bent in half, a tuna on the line for sure, and suddenly we had no more time for pointless noodling about life and its purpose, or lack thereof. There was a fish to catch. Finally.

****

Relative to the motel dwelling with Katie Ketchup, life with Rich was like living in a museum. Everything had a place, from the backup bed linens to the remote controls for his stereo system, which I could barely operate, to the car cleaning supplies he used to keep the BMW coupe looking brand new. Leaving a dirty fork or plate in the sink was a no-no. That's why I was cleaning dishes and vacuuming the house with Richie expected to return from a weekend of beach volleyball in San Diego in less than an hour.

"Thank God it's hockey season," Dad said by way of greeting when I answered my cell phone.

He was referring to Game 7 of the ALCS, in which the Red Sox run was squashed by a questionable managerial move.

"We'll get 'em next year," I said, amused that he was still capable of such disappointment over a team that did nothing but disappoint.

"No, we won't," he said.

"No, probably not."

"Can you believe he didn't pull Pedro?"

"I liked sticking with him, actually." I rested the phone between my cheek and my shoulder, scrubbing dishes, as Dad gasped at my response.

"Where did you watch the game? You got some buddies out there?"

"Didn't see it, Dad. I was fishing," I said.

"Fishing for what? You're kidding, right?"

"No, I'm not. How's Mom?"

I could almost hear Dad's disbelief, that his own son had been on a boat with the Red Sox a couple innings away from a World Series berth. This was, perhaps, the first time he began to realize that I really had broken free of Boston's gravitational pull, and it was a lot easier for that realization to come via my indifference to the Sox than to have to outline it for him explicitly. Neither of us wanted that.

"Good, Tommy. Real good. She misses you. Jimmy stopped by the other day. He's gonna paint the downstairs bathroom for us. No charge. Good kid."

I realized I hadn't talked to Garvey in over a month.

"That sounds about right."

"Yeah, good kid."

Dad once let Garvey sweat out an entire day and night in his jail just because Garvey took his cop car for a quick spin down Windward Way, lights and sirens and megaphone and all. Now, Garvey's a "good kid" and I hear, secondhand usually, that Dad still tells the story about Garvey taking the car, calling it 'the funniest damn thing he had ever seen.'

"Does he ask about me, Dad?"

"Who, Garvey? Sure, he takes the piss outta ya, you know how it is."

It sounded like Dad was on my side, like he wasn't participating in taking the piss out of the fancy California boy with Garvey. I enjoyed hearing Dad talk to me like a friend, less like a son, let alone a disappointing son.

"Good to hear," I said.

Chad Godfrey

"Mom put your article on the fridge next to the picture of your nephew. Which reminds me, you need to get in touch with your Uncle Bill. He asks about you every time we see him, so call the man, okay?"

"I've been meaning to, sorry, but, yeah, the writing's great, Dad. You like it?"

"Mom hung it on the fridge for her friends to see."

"Yeah, you mentioned that. You like it?"

"It's on the fridge, Tommy."

"I know, but – nevermind."

I would have killed to actually hear him tell me that he liked my work.

"What is it, buddy?"

"Nothing, Dad, alright. Glad it's on the fridge."

"What about the screenwriting? Any progress on that front?"

I was pulled in two directions: first, shock and delight that he'd actually asked about something I was doing, followed immediately by dread at the prospect of having to tell him the truth: that not much was happening on the screenwriting front and, further, I wasn't all that bothered by this fact. That actually I'd started to wonder if I really wanted to be a screenwriter at all. The impromptu hour on the set of "Charlie's Angels II" had planted the seed of doubt in my head, and that seed had sprouted and blossomed in the ensuing months, as I watched every hopeful and wannabe in LA continue the endless dance of aspiration and disappointment. That was the problem with Hollywood— no one was what they actually were. That barista isn't a barista, she's an actress. That bartender's just pretending to be a bartender; he's actually a

188

producer. And that clerk at the Gap? She's just biding her time until her directorial debut happens.

"It's going great, Dad," I said, and left it at that.

Voice

I had been digging with my axe for so long, night after night in my dreams, toying with the storage trunk from all angles, that I never expected anything new or exciting to transpire by the dream roadside. But then, after having had more or less the same dream hundreds of times, something new and exciting did, in fact, interrupt the normal routine. I popped the trunk and had a look at its contents.

"It was a boat," I told Laura that morning after I woke from my dream.

"A boat?"

"Well, a model boat. Like a toy. It was called the *Laura Anne.*"

"A toy boat, named after me? Quite an honor."

"I wonder what it means," I said.

"Wait, maybe it means we need to save up for a boat so we can sail around the world," Laura said.

In retrospect, this should have been my first warning that Laura was thinking about other places and things.

I didn't disagree that Laura was a major player in the dream but I wondered if the meaning of it all was deeper than that. After all, I had been digging in my dreams for a long time and didn't figure the lessons, if any, to come right out and slap me in the face like she was suggesting.

"Too small," I said.

The Pacific Ocean spread out below us as we drove north to Malibu on the PCH for dinner at Duke's. Laura had heard from the mother of one of her campers that Duke's had fabulous fish and chocolate cake and views of the ocean. My wallet was sure to take a beating, but I didn't care much.

"The boat was too small?" Laura said, turning down the radio to address my stupidity. "It was in a *trunk*. Of course it's too small to actually sail people. It's a model boat. It's a dream. It's a *symbol*."

I loved that Laura showed interest in me and my dreams and this whole synchronicity thing I'd introduced her to, but I hoped I hadn't implied to her that dreams are full-proof blueprints or life manuals. Maybe they are, but I sure didn't know that.

"It was a small boat," I said. "A day sailor. You could never get that boat past a wind-protected bay, let alone around the globe."

Despite its small size, the intricate beauty of the boat in my dream was remarkable. The hull was spotless, and although just a model, it appeared to have been washed and waxed with great care. Its sails were a kaleidoscope of brilliant colors and multi-faceted patterns. The wood was varnished and oiled and every inch of metal was polished to a sheen. The sun that hammered my back and shoulders reflected brightly off the fresh wax and metal on the model boat and gave it a glowing, heavenly appearance. It was perfect. I couldn't even hear the passing cars as I held the boat in my hands.

"Maybe Barney is thinking about starting a fleet and you'll end up running a boat for him," Laura said as we took our seats in a booth at Duke's overlooking the ocean. The view was spectacular but not spectacular enough to finally distract Laura from the boat dream.

"So the fish is good?" I asked her, tiring of the dream talk.

"That's what she told me, the salmon is delicious. I'm starving."

The waitress came, and we ordered wine and asked for bread. I put the menu down, happy to have spotted a mahi mahi dish that came with sautéed spinach and a side of garlic mashed potatoes.

"Speaking of Barney, you should see how he treats his boat," I said.

"Really?" she asked, still looking at her menu.

"It's incredible, cleaner than a test lab. It's like his child, his wife, his *lover.*"

"That's beautiful."

I wondered if Laura was my boat and if that was what my dream was trying to tell me, that I had worked hard to finally get to her, the treasure in the trunk. I knew that I had come a long way, that I had dug a formidable ditch in my own life. And Laura surely was a treasure.

The waitress arrived with our glasses of Pinot Grigio and I ordered the mahi mahi.

"I'll have the barbeque chicken, please," Laura with that knee-trembling smile. The waitress nodded and walked away, scribbling on her notepad.

"I thought we drove an hour for the fish," I said, knowing the chicken at Duke's was probably ten times as expensive but no better than what could be had at a restaurant near Redondo.

"I think it would be cool to work for Barney, don't you?" Laura asked. "When can I meet him, anyway?"

"You got chicken?"

"Yeah, barbequed. It comes with rice and pine nuts, yum."

Girls like Laura have nothing to hide, yet are difficult to ever totally understand. Their transparency is only illusion. I loved that. It challenged me.

"What happened with that Perkins lady?" I asked, convinced by now that the fish vs. chicken discussion was fruitless.

"Oh, yeah, she's offered to build us a new headquarters."

After my Kudos for Kids article published in the *Beach Times*, a lady named Johanna Perkins had come to Laura bearing gifts, money mostly.

"Wow," I said.

Laura purposely didn't pay much attention to money. It simply didn't interest her much. So it made perfect sense that she wasn't immediately quoting financial figures for construction costs or boasting about the ungodly amount of dough Mrs. Perkins could shower upon her.

"And she gave me this blank check to get some pencils and chalk and lab equipment and anything the kids need," she said.

"A blank check?" I asked.

Lucky for the world of nonprofits, Mrs. Perkins was keen on donating massive sums of cash to causes worthy of her great granddaddy's Texas oil and freight line fortune.

"Yeah, and the cool thing, Mrs. Perkins told Francine, the head of the whole program, that she wants *me* to take care of the money, to make sure the kids get all the best stuff. We had a connection, me and Mrs. Perkins, I think."

It didn't surprise me that Mrs. Perkins had fallen for Laura, too. Everyone did.

"Sounds like a good opportunity for you," I said.

"For the kids," she said. Of course, the kids.

Laura ate only two bites of her chicken but filled up nicely on my mahi mahi and garlic mashed potatoes.

****

Some writers like stylish laptops and coffee shops, others like poorly lit basements and Underwood typewriters. Me, I liked my big oak desk overlooking the distant waves and the surfers and the mid-morning sunshine. I used to prefer to write at night after a few cocktails or a bottle of wine and not before then. I still did that, too, but now that Laura was around, spending most nights with me at Rich's, I liked to save the bulk of my nights for her. Morning is relative, of course, but I tried to be typing by nine and into the office at the *Beach Times* by early afternoon. My tenure and credibility had grown in recent months so I often told them I was "out" and they didn't ask too many questions about my supposed research or out-of-office interviews I did in the morning. I'd stay at the *Beach Times* till around six then head home to meet Laura for dinner. Most days I squeezed in a Strand run or a lift at Impact Gym on Aviation at some point in between.

My days weren't carbon copies, but there were some patterns I fell into and liked. I'd wake up, shower, walk to Coffee Bean for an iced Americano, walk out the door of Coffee Bean, remove the lid of my coffee, turn back to the Coffee Bean so Freddy could redo my coffee correctly, and then I'd head home to my desk with an *L.A. Times* and a clear mind with a purpose.

As blowhard and flip-floppy as the sports writers were at the *L.A. Times*, reading them helped me get into gear to attack my own writing. When I wrote with a purpose, some emotion, my work was better. Somewhat contrived emotion it was, but it was emotion nonetheless and it helped. When the Americano was finished and the *L.A. Times* exhausted, I'd turn my baseball cap backwards and get down to business. I looked at the prospect of hammering out quality prose as my competition. I'd write for an hour then break for fifteen minutes to go the bathroom or do some push-ups or pace around the house. Sometimes I'd call home, but that usually took too long and distracted me too much from my work. I'd return to the laptop and the oak desk and do it again when my break was up.

I no longer thought about death and mounting bills and crashing planes and the wrong woman all the time. I still did think about these things occasionally, but I was clearly writing with a, well, healthier voice. My anxiety was behaving well. Maybe it was Laura, or maybe it was the

195

sunshine, or maybe the financial relief from my overpaying gig at the *Beach Times* had flipped the switch. I was banging out six, maybe eight pages a day of stuff that I thought made the grade. My characters were blossoming and the twists and tales of the spooky synchronous happenings were cause for optimism.

And what was more, I realized somewhere along the way that I was now writing for the right reasons—because I loved the story, because I believed in the characters, because the work itself had become the juice. Did I still want to sell a screenplay for a million bucks? Sure. But in an ever more distant, beside-the-point kind of way. I was aware that things had changed, that I felt better than I had in a long time, more content, more at ease. But I chalked that up to circumstantial things, rather than what it really was, what it turned out to be: a fundamental and permanent shift away from the directionless, scared-shitless young man I'd been when I first arrived in Los Angeles.

Writer's Dilemma

S ome days start better than others. Some days you know before you even get out of bed that it's going to be bad. And some days, you're lifting weights before heading off to college and one of your nuts rotates in your sack and you wind up in a medical office with a guy in a white coat fondling your chassis.

"It's a fairly straightforward case of testicular torsion," Dr. Shoenweiss said from his knees.

For me personally, having another man feel my nuts is awkward. A state of vulnerability unlike most others. The realest transfer of power I've ever experienced.

Shoenweiss chuckled to himself. "Though 'straightforward' is probably an unfortunate choice of words, in this case."

"Testicular what, now?" I asked.

"Torsion."

More fondling. More *hmm*ing and *uh-huh*ing.

"Torsion?"

"Tah-ore-shawn. You do heavy lifting, squats maybe?" he asked.

"I guess," I said, trying to process.

Dr. Shoenweiss patted me on my bare thigh and stood to toss his latex examining gloves into the biohazard box below the hand-washing sink. I happily pulled my boxers and jeans over my legs and waited for more things I surely didn't want to hear from the Harvard-educated Head of Urology at Beth Israel Hospital in Boston. "I've manually rotated your testicle back to its proper orientation," he said.

The dick Doc extended his fists in front of me and showed me what proper testicular orientation looked like – thumbs to the ceiling, pinkies to the ground. Mine was not normal, he explained with more hand gesturing. "But you will need surgery, sutures to stabilize the testicle in the testicular sack."

And that was that. Two days earlier I was healthy as a horse, and now I wasn't.

Even worse, for six weeks after the procedure, I had to wear protective underwear, or a "cock sling" as Garvey called it. (After he told the entire town, I suppose he had to call it something). Picture a jock strap with a big hole in the front.

The cock sling finally came off, but the pain never subsided. Not while I was wearing the sling, and not after.

"Common mistake," Dr. Shoenweiss said months later, again on his knees, back in power.

"Excuse me?" I asked, breathing through my teeth at the ceiling.

"Epididymitis. Not torsion. Or maybe you had torsion then, but this is epididymitis now."

Bullshit. This was the same exact pain as before. There is no "then" or "now." Nothing has changed. My left testicle was in the same elevated position and still throbbing, just like before. You blew it, buddy.

"Celebrex and Levaquin for a month should zap it," he continued aid with offensive optimism, tapping my thigh and removing his gloves.

"But I had surgery. Expensive surgery."

"No harm done," he said.

"But . . ."

"It's okay. These meds are real go-getters, you'll be fine now."

Now? Gosh, how trivial of me to feel a bit disappointed, a bit concerned that the last hope of continuing the Rafferty name may have been compromised. Whoopsie-daisies? Here's some pills?

Dr. Shoenweiss is not the only doctor who has failed me since I started paying my own medical bills. There was a Dr. Kline who treated me for a sore throat when it was walking pneumonia. Dr. Shue treated me for a pulled muscle when a later x-ray revealed a cracked rib. And don't even get me started on dentists. It'll be touch and go whether or not my first-born is owed to my dentist back home, Dr. Wienerman. It seemed to me that, by the time I was finally getting to the bottom of a health or dental problem, my body's own mechanisms could probably have fixed the ailment on its own. And it would have been a whole lot cheaper.

Misdiagnoses and out-of-this-universe medical bills had made me apprehensive about doctor's office visits. But the pain in my stomach was too much to take anymore. If my posture was one of those evolution visuals where monkey turns to man, I was *de*volving. My shoulders were beginning to bow forward like those of a skinny orangutan, one who occasionally reaches to his midsection to press and massage the daggers stabbing him in the belly. Laura suggested the Centinella Medical Clinic on PCH in Manhattan Beach. Quick and easy, she said from experience, and I had no choice but to give it a shot.

"How much do you drink on average?" Dr. Chow asked from his swivel chair against the panoramic window showcasing the mansions of Manhattan Beach surrounding his office.

The question irked me. My defenses were immediately brought to attention. Lying to a doctor could mean prolonged pain or misdiagnosis so I swallowed my dignity and crept slowly forward with a version of the truth.

"Per week?" I asked.

"Sure," he said, well aware I was stalling.

"Twenty."

"How many?" he asked again, perhaps knowing he'd get closer to the truth by having me repeat my answer.

"Thirty or so."

"Thirty drinks a week?" he confirmed and removed his eyeglasses to stare me down with a heavy dose of concern.

"Beer mostly. I know the hard stuff, like whiskey, is not good for you so I've cut that out of the diet."

"Beer is not the good stuff, Mr. Rafferty."

Speak for yourself.

"I didn't want to lie."

Dr. Chow scribbled some notes on his notepad and I knew I was about to hear some things that would be far from music to my ears.

"Gastritis," he said. "You have a whopping case of gastritis. Your stomach is red-hot. Your excessive drinking, the stress, the cigarettes, the greasy food diet are all aggravating your stomach."

"Everyone my age drinks this much."

"They don't. You have a relationship with alcohol that many do not have, in fact, and you need to address it," he said and pulled out a prescription notepad.

Dr. Chow prescribed me six months of Nexium and guaranteed me that drinking during the next year would cause permanent damage to my insides, perhaps erosion of my esophagus and a head-start on stomach cancer. Once I heard the "c" word come off his tongue, my stance changed.

Fucking doctors got me again.

****

When I thought of the arc of my efforts and ambitions as a writer, I thought of Clark Roddick, my high school English teacher. Clark was a really fine educator who cared more about my personal growth than any other teacher I ever had. Clark, to me, is frozen in time as a twenty-six-year-old original, a liberal but practical innovator who had no time for nonsense and didn't sweat the small stuff. Clark was the first authority figure who encouraged me to be more than a casual writer, which meant a whole lot to me, and in fact ended up being the first and primary influence that led me away from my long-standing ambition to be a doctor.

Clark taught me that no one was above editing, least of all me, and that rewriting and constructive criticism were natural, to-be-expected parts of the process. As such, he brutalized the stories I gave him, covered my creative writing samples in red marks, cross-outs, and all kinds of editing suggestions. And he did it all with words I understood. It wasn't "omit needless verbiage to enhance linear progression." It was "boil the shit down, Tommy, so I don't fall asleep." Whenever I ramble, or feel myself becoming too cute or otherwise in love with my own prose, I think of Clark and get to distilling. In short, whenever faced with the question of how good my writing was and/or how it could be improved, Clark was the first person who came to mind. And so, as I entered the office of Andrew Friedman, a book editor and another of Mrs. Perkin's beneficiaries, I thought of Clark again.

And I wondered, not for the first time since this meeting had been set up, why either Mrs. Perkins or, more to the point, Laura thought it would benefit a screenwriter to meet with a book editor. I had nothing to sell him, after all, and he probably had little to offer me. But here I was. I trusted their judgment.

"I understand you wrote a book," he said after the introductory chatter, where I learned most notably that he was an uprooted Mid-Westerner and the new proud daddy to Mrs. Perkin's first grandbaby.

"A script," I said.

"A script?"

"That's right."

"Why a script?" he asked.

"Why not?"

"Think about it, please, if you would. *Why?*"

"I like movies."

"What kind of movies?" he asked.

"Good ones," I replied, annoyed.

Friedman looked like a young Albert Einstein, or maybe a Larry from *Three Stooges*, or a short Bill Walton, Portland Trailblazers era. He was all hair.

"And what makes a good movie, Tommy?" he asked.

"A good movie doesn't try too hard."

Though I'd just come up with it on the spot, I liked my answer. It sounded informed.

"How so?"

"It takes a small bite instead of a full helping. A slice of life. A particular town, a particular era, very specific characters with very specific circumstances."

"For example?"

Rich and I had watched "Dazed and Confused" the night before and it fit the criteria.

""Dazed and Confused", for one. Small town Texas. A day in the life. A small group of friends in the middle of Texas in the late 70s."

"You liked it?"

"Loved it. It didn't strike me as an intended summation of a decade. It didn't get too preachy, try to wrap its arms around something as un-graspable as a generation or a massive state like Texas. We learned plenty, but we didn't get it stuffed down our throats. The clothes, the music, the vocab – it did enough on its own, set the stage, without interfering with a good little story. Horse and carriage were in order."

"The vocab?"

"McConaughey had some beauties, didn't he? Told us what we needed to know about the mindset of those kids in 70s Texas without being too explicit, offensive about it, you know?"

"Offensive?"

"To our intelligence," I said.

Friedman liked that.

"Any others?"

204

"Sure, many others."

"Like?"

"Well, there's plenty, come on."

"You like to watch movies, but why write them?" Friedman asked, and we were back on first base.

"I think it would be exciting, you know, to write one, to have . . ."

"Your name honored, a standing invite to industry ragers?" Friedman thought he had me pegged and I didn't like either his arrogance or his presumptuousness.

"Naw, I'll probably head back as soon as I sell one, actually." If I weren't confident about selling a script, nobody else would be.

"To Boston? To strut around town and brag to everyone who knew you when."

"I've done Hollywood and the whole dog and pony show ain't for me."

"You've done Hollywood?"

"West Hollywood, yeah. Sorta. I mean, I lived there, did some meetings."

Friedman liked that, too. I could tell by the way he pitied me with a nasally chuckle.

"You ever take a writing course?" he asked.

"Not really."

"Okay, well, one of the first things they tell you in class, the good ones do, is that you should trust your instincts. Your first instinct is your story, voila, the truth of it all. It applies to writing, and it applies to life.

The truth of it all, Tommy, is that you moved to Hollywood as a first inclination. Beach living came second.

"With all due respect, I moved to Hollywood because I had no idea where else to go, how about that?" I paused, the fiery side of me started to percolate in my gastritis-lined belly. "Why are you here? I thought all the serious book people were in New York."

Friedman hadn't been prepared to have his own psychobabble turned around on him, and this landed in a way he tried to hide, but didn't.

"We're here to talk about you."

I thought about this a moment, then offered the most honest answer I could come up with.

"I didn't know any better," I said, as if to avoid an after-school detention.

"I think you did, though. Besides, I don't sell movies."

"No?"

"I don't think you will, either," he said.

Friedman folded his hands neatly on his desk and looked me hard in the eye.

"Tommy, listen," he said. "If your primary goal was to make a good movie, maybe you'd have a shot, as good as their lottery odds will allow, anyway. You do seem to have a voice. But you don't need to make a good movie, as far as I can see. And that is your problem. The difference between 'want to' and 'need to' is all the difference in the world."

"Ok, then, what do you think I need?"

"If you want to write a book, we can talk," he said.

"A book?" I asked.

"Write us a novel," he said.

"A book?"

"A book."

Having had more than enough of that, I went for a stroll through the 3rd Street Promenade, not far from Friedman's Santa Monica office, to smoke and clear my head. The doctor wanted me to quit cigarettes, but cutting down was, for the moment, the best I could manage. No way I was giving up drinking *and* smoking at the same time; that was just unreasonable.

I hoped everything Friedman had told me would evaporate from my mind with sunshine and carcinogens, but it didn't. I was offended by his characterization of me, my supposed self-righteous intentions in particular, but he wasn't totally wrong. In fact, the more I walked and smoked and thought, the more I realized he was absolutely right.

Homeless people, street performers, and shoppers joined me in my confusion on the Promenade. I enjoyed the distraction the people provided and the chocolate chip ice cream cone I called lunch was quite refreshing. Ice cream still felt good. I thought of FarFar's Ice Cream back home after the beach trips. Great memories.

When my ice cream cone was finished in less than two blocks, I waited in line for a coffee at Starbuck's for ten minutes. It killed some more time and prolonged thoughts of Friedman's words a little longer. I preferred to watch people order their coffees and to avoid this new dilemma of what medium I would write in, how exhausting book-writing would be, or if I would continue to write at all.

Coffee and smoke in hand, I tried not to step in pigeon shit and the chewing-gum left on the pavement by careless people. I eventually stopped walking to watch a lip-syncing guitarist play some oldies. I wondered if anyone else noticed his electric guitar had no cord attached to it.

And standing there, watching this guy not play guitar and not sing, feeling every bit the fraud that he was, I realized I wanted very badly to do something I had avoided at pretty much every moment of uncertainty or crisis I'd experienced in my life: call my father and ask his advice.

"Hey Tommy," he said when he picked up, sounding distracted, as though maybe I'd interrupted him mowing the lawn or watching golf.

"Hey Dad," I said. That was all I could get out, in the moment.

"What's up?" he asked after a pause. "Everything okay?"

"Well," I said, "yeah, everything's fine. I'm not homeless and I'm not broke and I'm not dying."

"That's a good baseline," he said. "What's the problem?"

"It's that obvious, huh?"

"You were never good at hiding distress, son."

"Ah, I don't even know where to start, Dad," I said. "I'm not sure you'd want to hear it, or that you'd understand even if you did want to hear it."

"Stop worrying so much about what I'll think."

I took a breath.

"I'm not sure I made the right decision," I said. "Coming out here. Or maybe it's that I made the right decision, but for the wrong reasons."

"Well you know me, Tommy," he said. "I'm a simple man. Way I see it, it doesn't matter what got you there. You're there and doing ok, right?"

"I know," I said. "And that makes sense. But what if I told you I'm not sure I want to be a screenwriter after all?"

There was a pause on his end.

"I'd say I like the idea of a place where you can play golf 300 days a year," he said and shared a warm chuckle.

"That part is nice."

"Tommy, here's the thing," he said. "Maybe you want to write movies, maybe you don't. But you've got a good job and a good girl and you seem about as happy as I can remember you being since you were a boy. None of that sounds like the result of a mistake, not to me."

Plenty to think about. And I could manage to do that. I thanked Dad for the chat and he told me I was "on the right track".

'Ends' in Sight

*D*ear Tommy,

To be twenty-five again would be a blessing. My elbows and knees have forgotten their job descriptions. But I am happy, mostly, with what has transpired for me since I was that age.

Just prior to turning twenty-five, thirty even, I had already wasted a lot of time. I hardly remember most of my days when I was a twenty-something. You already know this, Tommy, so why bother mincing words: I was a drunk, plain and simple. I know the "waking up on a drug lord's couch in Colombia" story puts you in stitches, and I can laugh about it now, too, but those were truly hard times. I lost touch with my kids. My wife left me. I couldn't hold down any job or control my temper. I'm lucky I'm alive.

I loved architecture as a kid. If I wasn't playing hockey, I was doodling on the construction paper Nana bought me. I must have had plans for fifty buildings by the time I got to college. Fast forward thirteen years and I turned thirty with my architecture dreams surprisingly still in good shape. Clean and sober, family relationships mended as best as possible, I took a job as an apprentice of sorts for a local architect, Fernie Davis, and he showed me the ropes until I had all my skills and licenses in place. I was scared (embarrassed?) by my age and meager job title, but I went forward with my plan to be an independent architect and real estate developer. (I *distinctly remember my friend, Lenny, chuckling aloud when I told him I landed a job as an apprentice. These days he works for me, so who's laughing now, Lenny?) Fifteen years later and a whole mess of projects and conquered insecurities under my belt, I am tickled with my career and the second lease on life our family's love and faith has afforded me. The feeling of living clean and working on the career I love is simply awesome. Maybe like a breakaway goal at the Beanpot? (Sorry, the glory days still haunt me).*

Your grandfather, Pops, was a strong man, as I hope you can remember, though I know you were young when he died. I like to think I got some of Pop's traits (I know you have). He may be gone now, but his legacy still drives me, always has. You see, he had nothing but his family and his pride. He stuck by me, as he did all of us. Late night pickups in jail, DUI payments on my behalf, fistfights with his drunk son — always, always, always in my corner, Tommy. Pops understood that the human spirit can overcome anything this crazy world drops into a person's lap. My drinking and drugging were not exceptions. He never punished me. He just hugged me, threw me in the shower and told me to stay alive long enough to figure it out and enjoy my life. I regret my lost time, but I cherish the people who stayed with me from beginning to end. I know it wasn't easy on them — just ask your mother. I was alone in many ways at thirty, but I could still feel their love.

Tommy, when I heard you had bailed for California, I was nervous for you at first. I worried where your road may end. I think I know you well, and I feared you may have been boarding your own bullet train. I'm glad to hear that I can put those fears to rest. Your mom and dad tell me about your job at the paper and your beachside living situation. Atta boy! I'm not one for giving advice (being, most always, the one who needs it, even now), but let me leave you with something Pops told me before he passed: "Billy," he said, "life is what happens while you're dreaming it away. Live your dreams and lose the fantasies." I think he'd like what he sees in you today.

Anyway, I hope this helps you some, Tommy. Look forward to seeing you at Christmas.

Your proud uncle,

William McManus

It was Tuesday afternoon and my second Americano was nearly gone. Laura usually worked a full day but she'd decided to play hooky, and she rustled around in the bed behind me taking an afternoon snooze.

"Your typing is giving me a headache," she said in her knockdown-cute sleepy voice.

"It's my job, baby."

"I know, but I'm tired."

"We can't move to Malibu so you can order barbeque chicken at Duke's until I sell one of these things."

Laura was out of bed now. Her hands felt soft, like skin does in the morning, as she cradled my cheeks in her palms and straddled my hips at my desk.

"I got an offer for a job," she said.

Funny, I didn't hear any tremors.

"Great. New program?" I asked.

"It's not close to here, Tommy."

"No?"

She shook her head "no" and kissed me tenderly, like I was a Navy seaman leaving port for a very long time. Something was wrong.

"Africa," she said.

Suddenly, my script, my ocean view, the house in Malibu, and Uncle Bill's praise meant less than a grain of beach sand.

"Africa?"

"Relief work. Doctors Without Borders. Mrs. Perkins gave them some money."

I felt suddenly nauseous, the pain in my stomach instantly worse than it had been in weeks.

"It's not work," I said. "It's volunteering, Laura. And you're not a doctor. C'mon, that's no way to live."

"Actually, they're going to pay me very well."

"How?"

"That was a condition of Mrs. Perkins' grant."

My blood boiled. I immediately felt an urge to strangle Mrs. Perkins for her inconceivable recklessness with my heart. My walls were crumbling around me, onto me.

"What about us?" I pleaded.

"You're a complete man without me, Tommy."

A double-edged compliment at best. A personal appraisal like that had not been uttered in my universe in some time. I liked it, but it wasn't enough. I felt nauseous.

"So what? It doesn't mean I have to be without you," I said.

"I have to go to Africa, Tommy. I think about all the kids and their circumstances."

"You don't even know them! You've never been to *Africa*."

"I know. That's why I have to do this. To help them, to help me."

"Help you?"

"You're not the only one who needs to grow, Tommy. I need to find myself, to make myself who I am, just as much as you do."

I looked around the room, maybe knowing I might never forget the details of this setting for this conversation.

"This is it?" I asked.

"For a while, yes."

"This is *it*?"

"I'm sorry, baby. I thought if anyone would understand, it would be you."

"What I did and what you're doing are completely different things."

"Are they? You up and left Boston without warning, without a plan."

"I had nothing and nobody. I was looking for an actual life. You're running away from one."

"Tommy, please."

"I'm going for a walk," I said, grabbing my smokes and sunglasses off my nightstand. "I'll be back later. Don't wait around for me, okay?"

Laura began to cry, but in my anger and hurt I didn't give a shit. I hit the door.

The California sun was as bright as ever, but it didn't feel like freshly dried laundry or anything like it. The actors and actresses and nighttime restaurant workers played beach volleyball near the Hermosa Pier. Their laughter was so loud and fake and irritating. *Don't these people have something to do? Walk the dog? Take out the trash?* I realized now that Laura stayed home from work because she had already quit her job, not because she wanted to sleep in with me and have a bunch of sex and fall deeper in love. Her deceit hurt my mind. And what kind of woman offers an out-of-country job to another woman with a serious boyfriend? Did Mrs. Perkins enjoy wrecking homes?

"Stacy?" I said over the phone, as I took a seat in the sand near a vacant lifeguard stand.

"Hey, T," she said.

"Laura's leaving me."

"Oh, I'm sorry, Tommy. What *happened?*"

"AIDS. Poverty. Sub-par medical facilities."

"What?"

"Do I need to spell it out for you, Stace? Africa!"

"Laura is moving to Africa?"

I almost chucked my phone, then squelched the urge.

"Mom and Dad were married and happy by our age. All their friends were, too," I said.

"So? That was a hundred years ago."

"I thought I had it beat and now I'm back to the start."

"Tommy, maybe this isn't about you. She can still love you."

"And leave me?"

"Yes. She can."

"So what the fuck do I do about it?"

"What do you want to do?"

I thought of Mrs. Perkins and her little checkbook. "I better not answer that."

"Fight for her if you want. But maybe you need to let her go. If it's meant to be, she'll be back for you."

"And I sit and wait?"

"No, you don't. You stand up and live your life like a man, Tommy. *Come on.* You've done the hard part. How many people have the guts to leave home and move to Hollywood?"

"It wasn't guts, it was fear."

"Well, still."

"It was me trying to erase everything wrong with this world by shocking you and everyone else with a sneak attack. A fucking shortcut. A pipe dream."

"So?" Stacy asked.

"*So?* Have you heard of anything more selfish in your life?"

"A shortcut? Are you nuts? If what you've shown me is a shortcut then I am one stupid girl. *You did it.* You've got that cocky wink back in your eye, I just know it. I can't wait to see you in person again because I know I'll see that guy who would stand up to…whatever. I'm sure she's great. But, but… you are amazing. You are going to make some girl so happy, and it's Laura's loss. It is *truly* her loss. And look, I haven't moved an inch in years, probably never will. And look how far you've come? Shit, you were on suicide watch for two years."

"I *have* made some changes," I agreed.

"Good. So call it progress and keep moving. You're coming home for Christmas, right?"

Stacy was in a rush but I felt so much better after getting a little bit of her time to talk.

"I'll be home. Can't wait."

"Learn from this and you'll come out on top. Remember what mom says?"

"What?"

"Don't waste your time giving your heart to people who don't want it."

Laura was right. Stacy was here when I needed her.

****

After reading the note informing me of Claudia's death on my door from our mutual friend and neighbor, Gary, I took a minute to gather my overload of shitty thoughts and recollect the last conversation Claudia and I had before she died. The finality of it all shook me and I needed a glass of water. I could feel her lips on my cheek. Sitting gingerly back onto my couch, I tried my hardest to remember that Claudia wanted no tears or sympathy, because she would be floating above me with joints that don't ache and a full head of hair now. The best way I could honor her, she said, was to keep asking old ladies if they needed help with groceries and flashing my smile when I did so. I couldn't help betray her wishes, though, as I flopped my head into my hands and began to cry like a child. God, I missed Laura already. So much.

I had to write or I was apt to find a tall bridge and test my flying abilities. I grabbed a short stack of white paper from my printer and wrote longhand, journal style. For two hours I wrote about the fleeting nature of the things in my life, how standing on my own two feet was my destiny, perhaps our destiny, and a scary truth. Twenty hand-written pages, front and back.

I wrote through the night, and by dawn had the first chapter of what seemed to be a book. Some of the pen ink was smudged from my tears. The writing was more than just words and sentences and paragraphs. It was *me*. And I realized that Friedman, for all his arrogance and dismissiveness, had been right. Screenwriting was a means to a dubious end.

This kind of writing, on the other hand, was the end in and of itself.

Down There

I peered out the airplane window and focused on a strip of coastline that held Duxbury Beach where I had spent so many carefree summers. I could see my younger, fitter, more vibrant parents carrying Stacy and me into the water for an afternoon dip after a beach blanket lunch. I could see Jackie sitting on her chair behind us, smoking a cigarette with a smile, tanned and in her element. I could hear the waves cresting and crashing, see the sand and the gulls and the kites gliding on a steady summer wind. Dad throws a football at my face from ten feet to gauge my reflexes and gridiron potential. Mom smothers Stacy in SPF 900. On and on.

As we descended, I looked up from the coastline to see none other than the street where I spent my childhood. I could actually see the roof of the house where I grew up. I wondered if the new inhabitants of the neighborhood had kids running the streets with smiles as large as ours were years earlier. I wondered if there were moms and dads having wine at the kitchen tables after putting their exhausted kids to bed like mine did years ago. I looked for teenagers jumping out first and second-story windows, late for their rendezvous with friends for a night of smoking, drinking, laughing, crying, and loving. I couldn't see them, but I knew they were down there. That's the way it's always been down there. I couldn't wait to see my old world.

Stacy picked me up at Logan. We didn't say much on the short ride through the Ted Tunnel and into town. I was too fascinated with the recent construction from The Big Dig to talk. Occasionally, I would mutter "wow" or "holy shit" or "when did that go up?" as we passed new buildings and roads and tunnels that made a complete mess out of everything I remembered. Roads I had driven over a year earlier had been torn up and new roads were in their place. Where there was once an exit to my place on M. Street in South Boston, there was now a six-story frame for an office building. The "Seaport", I think Stace called it.

"You miss it?" Stacy asked as she blew smoke from a Marlboro Light out her cracked window. She was the loudest smoker, by the way, I had ever come across. Inhales and exhales were passionate moments.

I looked out at a crane that stretched up to an impossible height.

"I'm not sure," I said. "I mean, yeah, of course. But 'miss' doesn't really encompass everything I've felt about this place since I went away. It's more complicated than that."

"Stands to reason," Stacy said, sounding underwhelmed by my poetic waxings. She took another drag.

"Cold winter, huh?" I said.

"You have no idea."

And she was right. I had no idea what they had been going through and I felt like a traitor, or a fraud.

"How's California's weather, good?" And she had no idea what I had been going through, so we were back to even.

"Yeah, it's consistent. Usually beach weather."

"Lucky son of a bitch."

I was dying to see my parents, but Stacy had planned for my hometown friends to congregate that first night at Seapoint, which was fine with me. We bobbed and weaved our way through honking horns and cars covered in salt and sand. I couldn't remember the last time I had seen my own breath inside a car. It felt great, and weird, to be home.

We made our way into the bar. It was Christmas and the love was in the air. The Bruins were on the television above the bar, people played pool in winter jackets, and the scruffy-faced guys in the corner of the bar hollered and smiled when their eyes met mine. Nothing had changed. My friends looked and talked exactly like I remembered. They expressed their love roughly, rising to hug me and whack me upside the shoulder. Rob put some deep-track Van Morrison on the jukebox, and it seemed like I'd never left. Which was both great, and a little unnerving.

Gathered around a large booth in the corner of the barroom, we were all there. Stacy, Rob, Garvey, Leahy, Patch, Park, Berzerk, Switch, Gammo, Caitlin, Lis. I wasn't supposed to drink alcohol for another six months on account of my gastritis, which made me nervous—this was a hard-drinking crew.

"I heard the chicks wear those thongs to the beach out there," Patch said in my direction on his eighth pint. Patch had earned his nickname on account of somehow being covered in Poison Ivy for the majority of his childhood. Conversation usually took a turn for the worse whenever he opened his mouth.

"Haven't seen any," I said.

"You're an idiot, Patch," Garvey told him.

"You're boring, Garvey," Patch retorted quickly. "Why don't you paint a house and go to bed early like you do every night. Just because Tommy's home doesn't mean you have to stay out past ten."

"Tommy doesn't need to watch you two fight like little girls," Leahy interjected. Leahy was the voice of reason, the dispute stopper. Or at least he always gave a good effort to be that. A dash of bitter but plenty of sweet in there, too.

Patch gave Leahy the finger and me a tongue-out smile before leaving for the pool table.

"Park, I heard you've got a serious girl," I said across the table.

"Yeah, man. Right after you left. We're moving in together," Park said.

"Marriage?" I asked.

"Moving in together," he reiterated.

"Marriage?" Rob repeated, just to embarrass the shy guy.

"Moving in together," Park said firmly.

Park looked like a 70s throwback, like James Taylor in his 20s or Dennis Eckersley sans mustache. He talked slowly and with purpose. He always meant what he said and rarely needed to raise his voice. I always respected Park and considered him a true friend. I'd know him the longest of anyone.

"You got a girl, Tommy?" Caitlin asked from inside a cloud of her own cigarette smoke and hooded Bruins sweatshirt.

"No. No girlfriend. I had one. Didn't work out," I said.

"Was it that crazy bitch?" Switch asked.

222

Switch was uncomfortably blunt, but people usually just took it from him, owing to his tendency to freak out when challenged in the slightest. He was large and had spent a couple years in basic training for the Marines. I'm not sure how honorable his discharge really was, but that's his story and I don't recommend probing on it.

"Emily?" I asked.

"Girl's a herpe," Gammo submitted, fielding disgusted looks for his choice of words.

"Someone else," I said, "Laura. She moved to Africa."

"Why?" Berserk asked.

Bobby Brzek was a great, giving guy with a last name that just so happened to transform into a fitting nickname. Like the rest, he had very little filter on his words in current company. His new neck tattoo, a cliché shamrock of some sort, looked hideous, and it had occurred to me to point out that he was Polish, not Irish, but the opportunity hadn't yet presented itself.

"Help Africans," I said.

"Why?" he asked.

"I don't know, man. You'd have to ask her."

"Why don't people volunteer to help me?" Berserk asked.

Stacy retuned from the bar with two more pitchers and everyone slid their empty glasses forward for a refill. I chomped on the ice from my pint of water.

I told them about Hurst and Kevin Costner and Katie Ketchup and how alcohol and stress and gastritis had turned my stomach lining into a brick oven. Switch said that shit only happens to me, and I couldn't argue.

We talked about Patch's masturbation injury and how he still only had partial range of motion in his neck. We talked about Leahy's new car and his younger brother's call-up to the Bruins. We talked about the Britney Spears concert Gammo went to because he thought his little cousin had said Burning Spear, and he explained that it was a pretty good show in the end. We talked about the fix-up work Garvey was doing on his house and how it was ruling his life. The joint was dark, a little dirty, and smoky because, unlike in California, the right to kill yourself (and everyone else) with cigarettes was still honored in the Bay State.

We stayed until the bartender was finished cleaning and had to shut it down for the night. It was a new guy behind the bar who I didn't recognize, but he welcomed me back nonetheless and asked how California was treating me. After a short cab ride, we landed home safely at Stacy's apartment in Charlestown.

****

The pickaxe dropped to the ground from my hand. It looked as though I was done digging. It was raining and the ditch I had dug was working, functional. The continuous flow of water struck me as scenic, an endless stream, this circulation of life. Inevitable. Unstoppable. The trunk was open and empty. The *Laura Anne* was gone. It had sailed. This hardly surprised me. Synchronicity, after all.

Peering over the edge of my ditch, I marveled at the flowing water. I bent over and dipped my hand in. The water worked through and around my hand, unobstructed, unimpeded. My smile was gone, but I wasn't sad. I was resolved. A big project was done, a project bigger than me, I thought. I could see the ditch as a whole, from the outside looking in. The sun, the dirt, the pickaxe, the water, the cars, the trunk, were all in front of me. No longer was I stuck, digging endlessly without knowing why. I understood my purpose. I grabbed my axe and crossed the highway on foot. The cars stopped and let me pass. They had no choice: I wasn't stopping for them.

****

It was weird, and also nice, to wake up not hungover as all hell after a night out with my hometown friends. Maybe gastritis was providing the perfect excuse to not destroy my organs and mind, after all. I went into the kitchen and could hear Rob singing 'N Sync in the bathroom. The loner in me needed a minute to himself.

I slipped on my winter coat, zipped it all the way up to my neck, and pulled a wool ski hat down to my eyes. Everything seemed to fit so nice and snug. I nearly broke my back slipping on the last step out of the apartment, did a quick Road Runner sprint, suspended in mid-air, and regrouped with a few deep breaths. I'd forgotten that around here, in winter, you had to walk low to the ground at all times, because there was ice lurking everywhere from December until April.

I took the long way to Dunkin Donuts near the Shipyard to get a coffee and a breakfast sandwich, enjoying every familiar sight. The little things made me smile and slowed my heart. The *Globe* on a doorstep and a billboard for WBCN looming over the street, people bundled against the cold slipping and sliding down the greasy sidewalks. The coffee from Dunkin Donuts tasted just like the brilliant, sugary magic I remembered.

As I passed by the bank, I noticed the thermometer on the side of the building read 14 degrees. Multiply that by five and you'd have the weather on the same day in California. It felt oddly nice, though, to be using my coffee as a hand-warmer, walking head down, looking up through my brows to shield my eyes from the brisk breeze. Even in the bitter cold, the people who passed managed eye contact, even a smile here and there. It occurred to me that Laura would love this place, and my mood was such that not even that thought had any sting to it.

I got back to Stacy's and headed straight for my laptop. I had forgotten the battery charger back in California so I only had a few minutes before I would run out of juice. Still, I was thrilled to get back to my new material, the book.

When I sat down to write, my memory could still turn the corner onto Exit 2 on a Friday afternoon and head up Great Neck Road past Zachary's Pub towards Maushop Village near the Popponesset Inn where Jackie lived. These are images and times you don't easily forget.

I had decided the Cape and this community would be the home of Charlie Simmons, the protagonist of my new novel, *Down Here*. My life was not interesting enough for a readable autobiography, but I still wanted to write about the Cape and my own childhood, all of which was precious and interesting to me if nothing else. The vehicle to do this would be Charlie, a homegrown hero of sorts who loses his dream of playing professional baseball to an errant pitch that smashes into his temple. This one-time golden boy turned Cape Cod landscaper helps us see why his home is like nowhere else and why life, his and ours, is so complicated and beautiful.

"What 'cha writin'?" Rob asked as he leaned against the doorframe.

"Why are you naked?" I asked, forgetting, for the moment, all about my book.

Rob chomped on a Nutter Butter and crumbs fell to the floor. "Clothes are in the dryer. Accident last night," he said.

"Accident?"

"I smoked a pack of Reds. They reek."

I guess if you don't remember smoking a pack of cigarettes, or at least don't remember making a conscious decision to do so, it can be called an accident. I still had no idea how he played Division I hockey a few years ago with his mass intake of cigarettes (and weed). To this day, he smokes all day and night, and it doesn't seem to faze him.

"Your boxers, too?" I asked.

"No, I just like warm boxers."

I hoped Stacy wasn't home. She had known Rob for twenty years but I still didn't like the idea of him being naked in front of her so casually.

"What's this, the book?" he asked, standing behind me with his elbow on my shoulder.

"Too early to tell."

"Can I read it?" he asked.

"It's not anywhere near finished."

"You get me a coffee?"

"Sorry, my hands were full." And they were. I had my own coffee and a newspaper to carry. The timer buzzed on the dryer, signaling, I hoped, the end of his impromptu nudist colony.

"That's me," Rob said. "Bar tonight, eight o'clock?"

"Naw, I'll be down my parents' place tonight."

"Tell the Chief and your mother I said hello."

"Sure."

I paused a moment before saying it, knowing I was in the prelude to a sappy conversation.

"Rob?"

"Yeah," he said, turning back and apparently checking a testicle for bumps or something that caught his attention.

"Does it matter if shit's changed for me?"

"Not drinking?"

I nodded.

"Not in the least, kid."

"Y'mean that?" I asked.

"Buddy, it's one less person to buy a drink for and I bet half these clowns, including me, quit drinking some day."

Not for nothing, but I think he was right about that.

Over the Bridge

I could still taste the bubble-gum ice cream as it melted and dripped down my forearms. I could see Jackie in a pirate's costume smoking her cigarette and sipping Dewar's as I ate the ice cream. I could see my parents and their friends drinking boat-drinks on lawn furniture as I played with seashells in the yard. I could still feel the splinter that almost went clear through my foot at the Popponesset Inn. I could still taste the lobster rolls at the Raw Bar, a once-a-summer treat. All these memories, shared by thousands of other Cape Codders, were what I now wanted to write about. A glow of ideas sprinkled my mind as I sat with

Mom, Dad, and Stacy having a nice dinner of steak off the grill, my dad's specialty. Rare and chewy as ever, but tasty.

After dinner, my parents and Stacey sat on the couch and watched a *60 Minutes* segment on Abercrombie and Fitch's controversially raunchy Christmas catalog. It was snowing sideways, and as I walked out to my car to get my toothbrush I decided to go for a spontaneous ride in the near-blizzard. My old man's car was slow to heat up so I shivered and fidgeted with the radio dial as I waited for signs of heat. I listened to Lynyrd Skynyrd tell me about the importance of remaining a simple man.

Once the engine finally heated up, I put the car in gear and slid around the narrow roads, trying to remember how to drive in the snow. Coming around a corner I almost fishtailed into a telephone pole, and from that point on I kept it under 20, lest I should have to return to my parents' and explain to my father why I'd gone out driving in a blizzard in the first place.

After a while I found myself parked at Duxbury Beach in a small parking lot facing the water. I killed the engine and got out, bent my head to the wind, and started walking. Surely I was the only person foolish enough to be out in this mess, and I had no idea where I was going. But it didn't matter. I knew I wanted to be out in the storm, and that was enough.

Duxbury Bridge is the longest wooden bridge in the country, so it makes for an excellent walk, even atop a foot of snow and sheet upon sheet of gnarly ice. Below the bridge were the waters where I had spent so much of my youth, especially in the summers. This is where I learned that cops are slow in sand, and that worm fishing with a cooler of beers is about as much fun as you can have on a single afternoon.

I didn't even feel the cold as I stopped to peer over the side of the bridge and looked out over the Back River, where a series of marsh inlets gave way to fantastic waterskiing paths and bar-b-que pits. But there was also new construction, big houses and private docks, the rich divvying up amongst themselves what used to be free to all of us.

Duxbury was evolving from a haven for the American dream, with families originally from grittier places like Lynn or Melrose or Brockton, to a display case for new money. I heard some call it Deluxebury now. In the 80s, it was Drugsbury. Things had changed. Each child now had his own row of comfortable seating in the SUV. Each family had a fancy motorized dinghy to get to their new Grady White outboards. Like everyone says, it was different when I was growing up. What can you do?

We never had a cent to spend on anything but booze and weed and the occasional CD or concert ticket, and we worked like dogs landscaping or painting houses during the summers. But things like boats and the Back River awaited us at 4 o'clock in the afternoon when we could punch out and convene for a cooler of cold ones and hibachi burgers. We'd crack beers and pass the joints long past sunset. We'd eventually pick up our empty cans and slowly motor back to the harbor and our beds, only to get a few hours of sleep and do it all over again tomorrow. We had it made.

I watched the seagulls shiver in the frigid water below and my desires were as clear as the ice in which the birds rested. I had changed. My decision was made.

Dad was dozing in his La-Z Boy and Stacy was already in bed by the time I got back from my consultation with the Back River. Mom was wide-awake and ready to talk it out.

"When will you be home?" Mom asked. She'd already had a good cry with my news at dinner, and now she wanted all the information I couldn't provide, to ask all the questions I couldn't answer about why I was moving home and when.

"Soon," I said.

"How soon?"

"Well, I have to pack and tell Rich he needs to find a new roommate," I said. "And find my girlfriend, my ex-girlfriend now, and wish her the best, I guess."

"Why don't you bring her? Are you in love?"

"I love her, yes," I said.

"Oh, she *must* love you, Tommy, I can see it in your eyes."

"She's not coming with me, Mom."

"No?".

"Not now, no."

"Why not?"

"Work."

"Love finds a way, honey." She was still excited and I almost borrowed some of her chipper feelings.

"Good things come and then they go, Mom. That much I've figured out."

"Then you've learned pretty much all you need to."

"It's okay, though. Who says I can't look back on good things and smile instead of feeling shitty that they're gone?"

"Some things do have a place and a time, Tommy."

"One dream passed, now it's time to live the next one."

"What's that?"

"Being here."

"And writing?"

"I'm gonna write a book."

"We'll be thrilled to have you home, Tommy. But there's one thing."

"What's that?"

"Fight for this girl if you need to. Wherever you need to do it."

∎∎∎

I was learning what I wanted to fight for in my life. First came my own sanity and happiness. Selfish, yes, but entirely necessary in this world, if you asked me. I knew Laura and I would be happy and quite sane if we found a way to make our relationship work amidst this whole Africa thing. But could I be just as happy, maybe happier in the long run, if I returned home alone and made a life for myself, without her? Would she be happier to go her own way, too? Would she regret it, twenty years from now, if I convinced her to forego Africa and come back to Boston with me instead?

These questions had no answers, of course. Because we could only choose one path, and never know how the other would have worked out.

****

I hadn't been behind the wheel of a convertible before, and now I understood why people drove them so fast. I knew I was dreaming but went with it.

The wind cascaded through my hair as it passed through the open top of the sporty vehicle. I was *flying*. Spurning my normal right lane, defensive driving routine, I zipped down the left lane of the highway on my way to the Cape. My right arm locked onto the top of the steering wheel, my body slightly lurched toward the center of the car for optimal coolness, I marveled at the ditch on the side of the road. It was the same ditch I had dug with my own hands. It was the same ditch that had revealed that damn boat, the sign that Laura was leaving. The sun still shone bright and the cars were still cruising down the highway, yet now I was amongst them. I was not looking to the highway, watching the rest of the world as it zipped by. I was driving my own car; I was living my own life.

"Keep your eyes on the road, hotshot," Barney said from the back seat, "and let the road take you where it may. Just don't crash this son of a bitch."

THE MAKING OF TOMMY RAFFERTY

I couldn't believe Barney was with me. I never pictured him away from the ocean. I rubbed my eyes and looked harder into the rear-view mirror.

"Where are we going?" I asked.

"You're dropping me at the docks. You, you're going home."

Barney was destined for his boat, the thing he loved, the thing that gave him the most joy and the biggest canvas to live his life.

"Can I come?" I asked.

"No. The boat is my place. You have yours."

Right as usual, Barney.

I drove and I drove, as fast as the car go. No cops or speed traps in sight. I passed the Duxbury exit, then Emily Hutchinson, then Sun Valley, never touching the brakes. The next exit was for California, and I took my foot off the gas, briefly, then watched as the exit went by. The next exit was for Laura. I wanted to stop.

I slowed again and pulled my car into the right lane to get off he exit for Laura. I hit the blinker, slowed to 25 mph as the signage dictated—and then saw the exit was closed, boarded off, "Under Construction."

I had no choice but to keep driving.

****

Stacy had an important meeting at work out in Westborough, so Garvey cleared some time in his day to shoot me to Logan to get on the plane that would bring me back to California and the sunshine. Pulling up to the curbside check-in at American West, Garvey helped me grab my bags from the bed of his pick-up and offered a handshake.

"You're not coming back, are you?" he asked.

For once, Garvey was reading me wrong.

"I said I was, didn't I?"

"Yeah, but . . ."

"Then I'm coming back," I said.

"What about the girl?"

"She's going to Africa, man. There's nothing I can do about it."

"You could go to Africa with her."

"Not gonna happen, man. She's got her life."

"And you've got yours?" he asked.

"Yeah, I think I do."

"Well, then. Mission accomplished."

Garvey knew me better than I knew myself. If he thought I had found what I needed, I was in no position to argue. His opinion still mattered more than anyone's, up to and including my own.

"Thanks for the ride," I said.

Garvey just smiled.

Walking into Logan, I rubbed my arms for a little heat and stopped at the automatic entrance to turn back for one more look at home. I couldn't wait to get back and put down some roots.

Dad had slipped an envelope into my carry-on backpack while I was home. It was sealed with clear Scotch tape, so I knew its contents were special. I waited until we'd reached cruising altitude before opening the letter, almost holding my breath as I pulled out a few handwritten pages:

Dear Tommy,

Mom offered to write you this letter, but I knew this could be a good opportunity to tell you a little about myself. I hope that is okay with you. God knows I probably wouldn't tell you these things in person. I hope this letter suffices and you can excuse my tardiness in putting my thoughts on paper for you. I also hope my story helps you to understand your childhood, my parenting style and how proud I am of you and your sister.

Tommy, I did not have a boat growing up in Lynn. I didn't have a car in high school. I didn't get on a plane until I was twenty-seven-years-old. As a kid I wore my sneakers until my toes came through the front and scraped along the asphalt as I walked to and from school. Even then, it would be a few months until we had the money to replace them. Funny thing is that I didn't know any better and was happy with what I had. Everyone in the neighborhood had holes in their sneakers and spit in their eyes. We were a proud lot of people. That was Lynn. That was me. It still is.

It wasn't until college (paid for by yours truly) that I realized the world was bigger than Lynn. My freshman year roommate's family had a ski house up at Sugarbush Mountain in Vermont. I felt so silly visiting him there, because I didn't own skis and had nothing to do while everyone else did what the whole point of being there was. But I found that I wanted those things. When I met your mother, I really wanted those things — for her, mostly. I wanted to give her and you kids all those things I didn't have. This is a common story and there is surely no need for either pity or applause.

Chad Godfrey

When I turned twenty-five, I was a few years into life as a policeman. Two of my partners had already been shot. One quit, the other was DOA. Young kids with young families. I feared I was next. Coming home to my family was not easy, but it was the most pristine thing I had and I loved walking in that door. Your mother was an angel. You kids were well-behaved and appreciative. It wasn't easy because I had to separate the horrors of the job from the sanctity of my home life. I didn't mean to be selfish or overbearing with you and Stacy, but I needed to keep things perfect at home. Otherwise, I would have gone off the deep end.

Holding you in my arms, teaching you to speak and walk, or throw a baseball, were the highlights of my life. Watching you get ready for school gave me reason to put my .9 in my holster and go earn a paycheck. You may think I enjoyed it, but that is far from the truth. Part of my occupation was maintaining a stoic, tough-guy image, and that's all it was — an image. The real me had more questions and concerns about my life, things I am only recently admitting to myself and your mother.

To this day I wonder why I ever became a cop. Family Benefits? Pension Plan? Guaranteed work? Respect from the old neighborhood? I don't know, Tommy. I still don't have the answer. I wonder how life would be different if I went to boat building school in Maine like I wanted to. Gramps laughed at my plan and I was already in debt up to my ears. I went where I knew the money was. Perhaps another common story? Regret? Absolutely. You've heard me say "that's life" more than once. I have my boat now and that's good enough for me. When I was your age, I had other things to worry about.

I have known since you were a kid that you weren't meant to wear a suit and tie. You'd rather play in the mud and look up skirts than do your homework. You'll understand why I had to keep those parts of you in check. Your ability to reach others with your pen has not gone unnoticed, either. When you were eight I picked you up at the principal's office for writing that raunchy poem on your desk. Your teacher, Mrs. Willis, said it was the most creative, funniest writing sample she had seen in years, but wanted to know how on earth you had learned those words. I told her I would take care of it and I remember that I did.

Tommy, you are a grown man now. If there's one thing I hope to have taught you it is that a man or woman must earn their keep. Whether you are a banker, a writer, or a lawyer like your sister, the cream does not rise to the top on its own. That is what I have been trying to tell you, to find something that makes you want to put in the work. But I did not have the words at hand. I was never against you being a writer, though I know you thought I was. All these feelings are clearly my fault and I apologize.

I am a proud father. I am getting older now and can see it and feel it, but what is crystal clear is that I am thoroughly enjoy watching you at your age becoming the man that you are capable of being.

I love you with all my heart, Tommy.

Your father,

The Chief

The stewardess handed me some tissues when she saw my t-shirt was drenched in tears that had rolled down my neck.

THE END.

Chad Godfrey

THE MAKING OF TOMMY RAFFERTY

Made in the
USA
Middletown, DE